HAVOK
SEASON TEN

HAVOK: SEASON TEN

A Flash Fiction Anthology

EDITOR IN CHIEF
ANDREW WINCH

The characters and events portrayed in this book are fictitious. Any similarity to real persons, living or dead, is coincidental and not intended by the authors.

© 2024 Havok Publishing. All Rights Reserved.

"Gales of Song": © 2024 Rose Q. Addams
"A Mistake by Any Other Name": © 2024 Elizabeth Arceo
"Heart of Madness": © 2024 Erin Artfitch
"Shenanigans": © 2023 Deborah Bainbridge
"The Mender of Broken Things": © 2023 Emily Barnett
"Lament of the Phoenix": © 2023 P. J. Benjamin
"Peace": © 2023 Hannah Carter
"Laid Bare": © 2024 Teddi Deppner
"Lester's Business Venture": © 2023 Jim Doran
"Aqua Vitae": © 2024 Gretchen E. K. Engel
"The Dual Dragon Dilemma": © 2024 J. L. Ender
"Sphinx Industries," "No More Tears": © 2023 Abigail Falanga
"Reuben's Farm": © 2023 Winnifred Fritz
"A Fistful of Socks": © 2023 Jeff Gard
"The Lost City of Lyonesse": © 2024 Ronnell Kay Gibson
"Her Regular": © 2024 Sophia L. Hansen
"Relic Recovery League": © 2024 Rachel Ann Michael Harris
"A Brother's Love": © 2023 Andrew Hayes & Daniel Gomez
"Fountain and Fire": © 2024 Kat Heckenbach
"Bifrost": © 2023 Laurie Herlich
"Stairwell Troll": © 2024 Lauren Hildebrand
"Hades for the Holidays": © 2024 Hailey Huntington
"Prairie Dragon," "The Sword Still Within the Stone": © 2023 S. M. Jake
"Miss Kobe": © 2023 Kevin King
"Grounded": © 2023 Rachel Lawrence
"Lady Hood": © 2023 Jenneth Leed
"A Hole in Valhalla": © 2023 Pamela Love

"Unsinkable Heirs": © 2023 Morgan J. Manns
"Remember Me as Victorious": © 2023 Rebecca Morgan
"First-Time Driver": © 2023 Elizabeth Anne Myrick
"Seaflash": © 2023 R. L. Nguyen
"A Dying Phoenix": © 2023 Karyne Norton
"The Sea's Mercy": © 2023 Maia Rebekah
"Fire Bear": © 2023 Lincoln Reed
"Rydinger and the Wolf," "The Black Blizzard": © 2023 Andrea Renae
"A Peace of the Stars": © 2023 Victoria Roberts
"The Path to the Sea": © 2024 Mia Rumi
"Waking Ugly": © 2023 Kez Sharrow
"The Santa Dilemma": © 2023 Nate Swanson
"The Collector": © 2023 Michael Teasdale
"Reginald's Saturday Morning Surprise": © 2023 Rachael Watson
"Not Too Late": © 2024 Andrew Winch

Cover illustration by Kirk DouPonce, DogEared Design
Cover typography by Jenneth Leed

Any unauthorized copying, translation, duplication, importation or distribution, in whole or in part, by any means, including electronic copying, storage or transmission, is a violation of applicable laws. No part of this book may be used or reproduced in any way whatsoever without written permission except in the case of brief quotations embodied in critical articles or reviews.

For information, contact Havok Publishing:
https://gohavok.com || publishing@gohavok.com

ISBN: 979-8884244030 (print)
First edition May 2024
Printed in the United States of America

CONTENTS

Introduction 1

LEGENDARY CREATURES

Lester's Business Venture / Jim Doran 5
Lament of the Phoenix / P. J. Benjamin 9
Stairwell Troll / Lauren Hildebrand. 13
 Reuben's Farm / Winnifred Fritz 17
A Fistful of Socks / Jeff Gard 21
The Mender of Broken Things / Emily Barnett 25
The Dual Dragon Dilemma / J. L. Ender 29
A Dying Phoenix / Karyne Norton * *READERS' CHOICE* . . . 33
Sphinx Industries / Abigail Falanga. 37
Prairie Dragon / S. M. Jake 41
Shenanigans / Deborah Bainbridge. 44
A Brother's Love / Andrew Hayes & Daniel Gomez. 48

LEGENDARY LOCATIONS

Lady Hood / Jenneth Leed 54
Fountain and Fire / Kat Heckenbach. 58
Rydinger and the Wolf / Andrea Renae 62
Waking Ugly / Kez Sharrow. 66
The Lost City of Lyonesse / Ronnell Kay Gibson. 71
Remember Me as Victorious / Rebecca Morgan 75
The Sea's Mercy / Maia Rebekah 79
A Mistake by Any Other Name / Elizabeth Arceo. 83

LEGENDARY THINGS

Bifrost / Laurie Herlich. 90

Relic Recovery League / Rachel Ann Michael Harris 94
No More Tears / Abigail Falanga 98
A Hole in Valhalla / Pamela Love 103
Aqua Vitae / Gretchen E. K. Engel. 107
Fire Bear / Lincoln Reed 111
Seaflash / R. L. Nguyen 115

LEGENDARY EVENTS

The Collector / Michael Teasdale 121
Laid Bare / Teddi Deppner 125
First-Time Driver / Elizabeth Anne Myrick 129
Reginald's Saturday Morning Surprise / Rachael Watson 133
Miss Kobe / Kevin King. 137
The Sword Still Within the Stone / S. M. Jake
* EDITORS' CHOICE **141**
Her Regular / Sophia L. Hansen. 145
Peace / Hannah Carter 150

LEGENDARY PEOPLE

Grounded / Rachel Lawrence 157
Hades for the Holidays / Hailey Huntington 161
A Peace of the Stars / Victoria Roberts 165
The Path to the Sea / Mia Rumi 169
Unsinkable Heirs / Morgan J. Manns 172
Not Too Late / Andrew Winch. 176
Heart of Madness / Erin Artfitch. 180
The Black Blizzard / Andrea Renae 184
Gales of Song / Rose Q. Addams 188
The Santa Dilemma / Nate Swanson 192

ABOUT OUR AUTHORS 197

For all those living life with big dreams, and with appreciation for the legendary dreamwalkers who have come before us

Special thanks to our Patreon supporters

Firebrand: **Olivia Gratehouse**

Faithful Sidekicks:
BashCoder Reptiles
K. A. Cummins
Andra Marquardt
Caleb & L. G. McCary
Steve Rzasa
Chad Statton

INTRODUCTION

"**R**ebirth isn't just a theme. It's a legacy."
That quote is taken from Havok's very first anthology, published five years and ten seasonal contests ago. And since then, our rebirth has indeed become a legacy. In the past five years, we've doubled our volunteer staff (to over fifty strong now), published over 1,400 stories, and provided a launchpad for hundreds of promising writing careers in an industry that's struggling to find its way in a swiftly changing world.

That's why we chose the theme of this tenth anthology to be Legendary. We wanted to challenge our writers to write stories capable of standing the test of time—capable of being remembered alongside the greatest tales chiseled into literature's enduring history.

And they delivered in a *big* way.

Spanning the genres of mystery, suspense, science fiction, fantasy, and humor, the stories you'll find here were carefully selected from six months of submissions and are packed with unforgettable subthemes of legendary creatures, people, locations, things, and events. From the seemingly mundane to the overtly epic, our authors have held nothing back.

But we would expect nothing less from a tribe that has boldly stepped forward and come alongside our journey these past ten seasons. Some have been submitting from day one, growing and sharpening their skills until their stories are among the best we now publish. Others are new to Havok and are already showing huge potential. And all of them share our passion for the written word. For exploring and harnessing universal themes that speak to all of us. For crafting impactful flash fiction that resonates long after that final punctuation mark. And that passion has become the spirit of everything you'll find within these pages.

From the unspoken heroes among our volunteer staff and unwaveringly loyal community to the world-famous authors and artists who have donated their time and brilliance to our cause (including the epic cover of this anthology), Havok would be nothing without its supporters. And that includes *you*. Every anthology delivered, every T-shirt sold, every story submission, every reader vote, comment, share, and conversation, allows our writers to keep writing and our readers to keep reading. And *that* is the spirit of the anthology you now hold in your hands.

So read on, and enjoy the journey. We certainly have. Because Havok's rebirth hasn't only become a legacy—it's become *Legendary*.

Andrew Winch
Editor in Chief

LEGENDARY CREATURES

LESTER'S BUSINESS VENTURE

Jim Doran

When facing a monster, espionage missions don't have to be lethal.

Hopefully this is one of those times, Secret Agent Rebecca Edelweiss thought as she knocked on the cabin's entrance. She squared her shoulders and put on her *I mean business* face while waiting for the creature to answer.

A bushy-haired, seven-foot man with rugged skin and eyebrows extending halfway up his forehead answered the door. His plaid shirt stretched across his muscular stature, towering over his five-foot-five visitor. Rebecca—with her professionally styled hair, red suit jacket, and gray pressed pants—stood tall in his shadow. She poked him on the breastbone. "Remove the disguise, Lester."

Lester rubbed his square jaw. "What *are* you doing here, Rebecca?"

Always the same question. As if they didn't know.

Rebecca didn't wait for his invitation and brushed past him, entering Lester's mountain cabin. She detected a pine scent and a moist earthy smell.

Shutting the door, Lester adopted a sarcastic tone. "Won't you come in?"

Rebecca noticed a package containing small plush toys next to the door. "You know why I'm here."

Lester stiffened, then eyed an adjacent kitchenette. "I only now put on tea. Take a seat."

Rebecca walked to the small table while Lester made for the kitchen counter. She selected a seat with a view of the cabin's owner. While she didn't expect him to run, she couldn't be too sure. Her eyes darted to the fake family photos on the walls and the porcelain knickknacks. The setup screamed domesticity. "You have a cozy place here, Lester."

He returned with the kettle in one hand and two teacups in the other. His cup had an oversized handle. "Thanks."

"Though you shouldn't be living here at all."

He placed everything he was carrying on the table. "Beats a cave."

Lester chose a chair that groaned under his weight. Rebecca pulled a doily close to her seat. "Did you make the mask?"

Lester huffed. "Mask! I'm insulted! I would think you secret agents would recognize prosthetics. The process takes hours to apply."

Lester set a teacup, spoon, and a variety of teabags in front of her. With his bare hand, he grabbed the base of the kettle with steam flowing from its spout, then tipped hot water into her cup.

Rebecca examined the tea bags. "Nice selection. Nice house. A little too nice for a yeti's salary."

Lester lifted his teacup with his beefy fingers, pinky extended. "I recently came into money."

Oh come on! "Yes, selling merchandise about yourself. What a setup."

Slurping, the yeti peered at the woman over the cup's rim. "Oregon has not outlawed capitalism... yet." He furrowed his brows. "That reminds me. I need to register to vote."

Rebecca used the spoon to agitate the water. "The head office sent me here. Normally, I'm asked to retrieve rogue creatures, but in your case, I'm here to demand you shut down your website, Lester."

"Oh, Rebecca, be reasonable. The store's not hurting anything."

She pointed at him. "You're selling T-shirts of yourself with 'Have you seen this beast?' and 'Oregon's Most Wanted.' Your job is to hide, not draw attention."

Lester waved at her, shooing away her objection. "No one believes it."

"Tourism in the area has increased forty percent." Rebecca tapped her spoon on her saucer. "You're not fooling anybody, Web Admin B. Foote."

Her host grinned, displaying his jagged teeth.

Time to switch tactics. "This isn't only about you. Shandlai had her foal yesterday. Six months from now, the nub on her head will sprout."

The yeti reared back in surprise. Thought so. He didn't know.

Slumping his shoulders, Lester hung his head. "I wasn't aware. I'll visit Shandlai tonight."

"Your duty is to keep people away from those unicorns." *Now to change my tone to Disappointed Mother.* "What happens when some tourist discovers them?"

Lester shifted, and the chair groaned again.

Rebecca rapped her knuckles on the table. "What if they're captured?"

Lester set his cup on the yellow, flowery doily. "You've made your point. Tell the office I'll resume terrorizing the countryside tonight. But Rebecca, must I take the website down?"

Rebecca sipped her tea. "Not my call. But you know what the office will say."

The yeti bit his lip, then beamed at her. "I guess it's not so bad."

Uh oh. Rebecca took a deep breath. "What're you scheming now?"

Lester spread his hands as if flattening out an invisible banner on a wall. "A going-out-of-business sale."

LAMENT OF THE PHOENIX

P. J. Benjamin

Easing my pale arched wings through the insistent wind, I watch the Last-Spoken far beneath me. Soft-skinned bodies frolic on the warm sands. They drift and splash in the teal waves that crest around them. On a day this clear, little separates the blue of the sky from the reflection coloring the watery expanse that falls away behind me.

I watch, and I remember the Speaking.

How many lives have I lived? Less, at least, than my rotations around the sun. Yet they cannot be counted, not using every grain of sand below to mark their place. Have I forgotten any? Would I know it if I have? I am not like the Speaker; I have a beginning.

But lives spent without eyes were but memories of thoughts. They held little sensation beyond movement and nutrition. I lived many such lives in the first moments of the Fifth Day. With each death, I added something to myself as the Speaker had taught, but who could say how many lives passed until the subtle shifts in my form granted sight?

I angle my wings south to match the humid air rising from the industries of the Last-Spoken. I am over their harbor town now and can hear the beasts of my current form wail among distant rocks. How long will we cry? The grief, the example we set by it—how can the Last-Spoken prance and play in ignorance?

The beasts know me. I have always been their shepherd. Charged by the Speaker as the firstborn of the Fifth Day, I guided them from the morning of deep water into the noon of shallow reefs. As evening came, I was the first to bring them onto land, to teach the breathing of air. In the twilight hours, I heard the Speaker bring the Fifth Day to a close. I listened from a mountain peak, learning I would never return to the water.

I stretch my webbed feet at the memory—how it itched when I finally hardened my scales for land!

Yet, my time as a Hard-Scale is one I remember fondly! Those lives spent before the noon of the Sixth Day were filled with radiance and warmth. The world smelled different, sweet and expectant. The air perfumed with a hint of the Days to come, for the Speaking had not yet finished.

As lives passed, my flock of beasts became titans in the empty land. They reached for the heavens until their necks burst above the forest's canopy. In honor of such holy desire, I sought to lead them into the sky itself, and so induced my first feathers. Today mine are pale and subdued, but those first were iridescent! I was a Hard-Scaled, yet fledged in shimmering hues of crimson over my hide's muddy green.

I had barely learned to use them when the Meteor fell.

Oh, the roaring it made as it fell from the sky above. A star plucked from the firmament! It struck the land with a force that shook the earth like a bell, a toll marking noon for the Sixth Day. Endless clouds of ash masked the sun while the fiery blood that veins the deep earth destroyed the verdant land. When the eruption stilled and rock cooled, what remained of life whimpered against the cold of endless shade.

So many beasts died in those first hours of ashy cloud and bitter cold. I called out, asking the Speaker to grant me the heat of the deep earth to warm them while hair replaced scale. In his kind allowance, he spoke a word of my very own, one I cherished in my heart. With that utterance, the ground burst beneath me and I flew into the air at last!

I became the fire-fledged bird, and until the twilight of the Sixth Day, the warmth gusting from my wings protected the development of those devastated beasts. In time, the ash clouds settled from the sky and the sun returned to radiate its glory. Only a few Hard-Scaled beasts remained. Hairy-Eggless filled the earth now. At midnight of the Sixth Day, the Speaker spoke his final word, and with his exhalation, the Last-Spoken rose from the dust of the ground.

Never had I seen a creature like him. Noble and valiant, he gave titles to each within my precious flock. I, too, was entitled. Phoenix, he named me, a name I bore until the time when forty days of rain claimed all but a few of the Last-Spoken. Only my legend remained, embedded in their imaginations as they filled the earth. Did they know the cycle of my rebirth foretold their own? Foretold how all things would be restored to true life?

Today, as my wings take me farther inland, I still cry at the memory of that life. How had things gone so wrong? The Day of Rest had only just begun! Even now, the recollection chars my heart black, though I had left my fire behind long ago. I had watched, knowing it was my place to see, but not speak, as the Last-Spoken failed to listen to the Speaker's words. And how, in scandalous humility, the Speaker arose from his Day of Rest to give them new words, words for those who failed to listen.

But that was long ago.

Miles inland now, the heat from a hill of hot trash keeps me aloft. Will I ever take another form? I do not know. I can only hope to mimic the humility of the Speaker; to show the Last-Spoken what they have made of the beasts I guide.

I tense with revulsion and dive from the sky. Alighting on the plastic mountain with the beasts of my form, I shriek my gull cry into the sunny sky. Eating the dregs of the Last-Spoken's waste, I weep, and I wait.

Wait for the Day of Rest to dusk and for the Eighth Day to dawn.

STAIRWELL TROLL

Lauren Hildebrand

"Pivot! *Pivot!*" Maddy shouted from under the aluminum ladder.

"For the last time, it won't *pivot*. We need to lift it over the stair rail to get around the corners." I rested my end on the iron banister and eased the duffle strap from where it was removing circulation in my shoulder.

Maddy's wild curls poked up between the rungs, and she gave me a sharp-toothed grin. "That you don't get the reference is just more proof you're a rural hick."

I sighed. Leave it to Maddy to quote some TV show or internet meme at the worst time. "Can we get the ladder downstairs already?"

"Sure, fine, waiting on you." She flicked her pointed ears—we were on a waning crescent, so she was down to just wolf ears, a tail, and disturbingly sharp nails and teeth—and vanished beneath the ladder. "On three. Onetwothree *hup!*"

I lifted my end and began the waddle-stagger of trying to carry an unwieldy item down stairs. The ladder shouldn't have been such a monster, but it had gotten stuck extended after a particularly harrowing wolpertinger extraction. And ever since my truck's toolbox was broken into, we'd been keeping equipment in the office's spare room. *And* since we were behind on rent again, we were currently sneaking up and down a claustrophobic, hospital-green back stairwell rather than going through the lobby.

Basically, inconveniences had added up. Paranormal pest extermination at its finest.

Maddy reached the next landing and hoisted the ladder up to clear the railing. Its foot swung the opposite direction and caught me in the stomach. I grunted.

"Hold up!" I shifted my grip, and the heavy duffle dug a new groove in my spine. We cleared the corner without doing noticeable damage to the walls and staggered on.

"Halfway!" Maddy yipped.

"Yay."

"You shall not pass!" a deep, bass voice bellowed up the stairwell.

Maddy dropped the ladder and spun into a fighting stance. The sudden weight yanked me forward, and I staggered. The ladder's feet kindly punched me in the ribs, keeping me from sliding face-first down the non-code-compliant stairs with fifty pounds of fairy traps on my back. I expressed my gratitude with an *"Ung."*

"Who's there?" Maddy snarled.

"None shall descend without paying the toll!" The voice echoed between concrete walls.

"Show yourself, Gandalf," Maddy shouted. "We have every right to use these stairs. I'll fight anyone who says otherwise."

I moaned. *It's only Tuesday. I was hoping the beatdowns could wait until Thursday.*

Scraping claws sounded below. "You think *you* can best me?"

I sighed. *One of those weeks.* "What do you want, master of the stairs?"

"A toll!" the voice boomed.

I shut my eyes. "What *kind* of toll?" My ribs had finished

registering their complaints, and my ankles were now chiming in. "Do you have a riddle to solve? Or need a gold piece? Or maybe you'd like to suck the marrow from our bones before sending us along."

"Um..." the voice faltered. "One moment."

Gravelly whispers drifted up the stairwell.

Maddy wrinkled her nose. "Trolls," she hissed. "I smell three of 'em."

"Great. They must've just moved in."

"If there's only three, I can take 'em!"

I eyed the petite teen. "Not on a waning crescent. You're mostly breakable human."

She sighed dramatically. "And it's *so annoying*."

"Yeah, tell me about it." I rubbed my elbow.

The whispers cut off. "Okay, we've decided gold is good, marrow is better, but you can pick. What'll it be?"

"How about I tear your tongues out and stuff them down your throats?" Maddy snarled.

"Ignore her," I called, then hissed at Maddy, "and give me a second to think."

"Why? We don't have gold lying around, and I'm not in the mood to get eaten today."

"Hey." I snapped my fingers. "We still have that possum carcass in the truck bed? The one we used as wolpertinger bait?"

"Yeah, Andy wouldn't let us bring it into the office."

"Okay," I called, "we'll pay your toll with marrow, but you don't want ours or we can't feed you again."

"Then whose?" The voice sounded confused. "You cannot pass without paying."

"Oh, we'll pay. And as a gesture of good faith, I'll leave my friend here while I fetch the payment. I just have one condition..."

I limped back from the parking garage, holding the stinking gunnysack at arm's length. At the base of the stairwell, three trolls—clearly a father, mother, and young whatever trolls call their offspring—peeked furtively around the doorframe. They eyed the sack greedily and licked blunt teeth. The largest reached for the bag.

"Wait." I swung it back. "You agreed to give all three of us safe passage."

The troll muttered something, but he and the female trotted up the stairs and returned lugging the ladder. Maddy followed.

They dropped it and held out leathery hands. "A deal's a deal."

"It is indeed." I passed over the noxious bundle and looked away as they tore into it, likely eating as much gunnysack as possum. "So, one piece of meat in exchange for each use of the stairs?"

The father troll nodded. "And we carry the metal torture device up or down so you can carry the payment."

"Precisely. It's been a pleasure." I jerked my head toward the truck. "Maddy?"

She snickered and grabbed the ladder, and we left the troll family to their putrid feast.

"So... we get to collect roadkill from now on?"

I sighed. "I'm leaving that delightful task to you and Lara."

"Yes!" Maddy pumped her fist. "There's a squashed cat over on Fifth. Suppose they'll notice a few bites missing?"

I gagged. "Do what you must. Just *don't* tell me about it."

"What's not to like? Custard, good. Jam, good. Meat, *really* good."

I stared blankly at her.

"And this is why you're the Ross of the group." She cackled and clambered into the cab.

REUBEN'S FARM

Winnifred Fritz

Once more, the sun set on Reuben's farm. Beneath the fuchsia sky, no kittens mewed, no cattle lowed. Eerie quiet filled the chicken coop, the barn, and even the doghouse. Not even birdsong broke the farm's unnatural silence. To the east, however, the world began to stir as sunlight left its skies. Living creatures would have shuddered at the maddened moans in the dark, but there was no life to hear it on Reuben's farm.

At least, not on the surface.

The creatures had destroyed most of the farm in the early days. Reuben had only been able to save a handful of animals, tucking them away in his bunker. Even now, the memory of those who had ridiculed him made him shake his head. "Prepper," they'd sneered. He'd been prepared, but where were they now? Wandering the night as mindless creatures whose base instinct was to kill, while Reuben was safe in his bunker.

The thick walls muted all outside sounds, but Reuben's security feed had audio. After tending the cow and chickens, Reuben settled down in front of the monitors with his dog and a cup of coffee. He kept the volume low. Wasn't much point in listening to the groaning of what the news had called "zombies," but Reuben craved connection with the outside world. His security feed was all that was left.

As far as he knew, he was the last sane human in existence. All alone, save for his animals' company. People and their chatter had always bothered him before. He had never thought he would *miss* conversation.

"Wish you could talk," he told the dog, stroking her head.

A high-pitched scream crackled over the feed, and the dog barked. Liquid scalded Reuben's hand as he jerked in surprise. Ignoring the burn, he scanned the monitors for the source. Had he misheard? Zombies streamed past the cameras, swarming in response to the sound.

Another scream had him jumping to his feet and making sure his Kimber was secure in its holster. Rushing to the exit, he fumbled to open the interior door. The dog tried to follow.

"Stay!" he ordered.

Another scream echoed through the speakers, and terror speared through him. Too slow! He was moving *too slow*! Reuben wrenched open the door, stumbled through, and shoved it shut behind him.

Wait. He paused before the exterior door. Danger, maybe even death, waited beyond. Why should he risk his life for a stranger? His cautious and reclusive nature was the reason he had survived in this new world. The shrill cry replayed in his mind. Could he really leave an innocent to the mercy of the creatures?

No.

He reached for his gun, prayed that there were no zombies in the immediate vicinity, and opened the hatch cautiously. To his left, a zombie veered toward him. Fast as a snake, he fired, hitting right between the eyes.

Guilt hit him like a punch. They might not act like people anymore, but they still looked human. Reuben whipped his head around, searching for the source of the screams. Several floodlights highlighted more zombies drawn by his gunfire.

"Where are ya?!" he called. "Make some noise!"

"Help me!"

Reuben veered toward the barn. Was that a little girl?

"I'm comin'!" Racing in the child's direction, he shot at the zombies lurching toward him, trying to aim away from the screaming. His aging body was not as spry as he would have liked, but he was still fast enough to outpace the clumsy oafs. *Almost there.* His first mag ran dry. Eject, reload, release the slide, fire again, again, again. Hit. *Miss.* Reuben could see her now. A tiny girl stood in the hayloft's dark opening, waving her arms and hollering. Zombies milled in front of the closed barn doors, too simpleminded to try to find a way inside. He wondered how the girl had managed— Oh! His eyes snagged on a hole in the barn wall, too small for the zombies to use.

"Hang in there, sugar!" he called, shooting zombie after zombie. There were so many! Even more closed in from behind, drawn by the racket of her wails and his gun. A hand caught his shoulder. He shook it off, tripped, tumbled to his knees. Back to his feet. *Don't stop!* He was almost to her, almost to safety.

Felling the last zombie in his way, he unfastened the rusty latch and slipped between the barn doors. Creatures lurched in behind him. The girl's cries halted abruptly, frightening Reuben more than the mindless creatures. He lunged for the ladder, relying on memory in the blackness. Could they follow? He reached the loft, turned, and strained to see into the darkness. The creatures bumbled about below, reaching, grabbing, but not climbing.

Scanning the loft, he bit back a yelp of alarm when the child flung herself into his arms and sobbed. Reuben caught her shoulders, quickly scanning her arms and legs. "You bit?" he barked. She shook her head rapidly. No.

Sagging in relief, Reuben drew the little girl close and tried to catch his breath. The child continued to cry with quiet, hiccupping sobs.

"There, there," he grumbled. He didn't know a thing about kids, but he *did* know how to calm a frightened animal. It couldn't be much different. His calluses caught on her matted hair as he gently stroked her head. "You're safe now, sugar."

Reuben wondered how such a little thing had ended up alone. He had a million more questions, but none of them felt important right now. They were both safe. That was all that mattered.

"You did good, kid." The praise felt foreign, but right. "They can't get us up here. They'll go away if we're quiet. Then we'll go home." They could figure out the rest later.

"Home," she whispered, her eyes wide and awe-filled.

Reuben's heart squeezed.

He wasn't alone anymore.

A FISTFUL OF SOCKS

Jeff Gard

His meticulously planned caper at Footsie Rolls Novelty Sock Emporium was off to a poor start. Crouched behind a sneaker deodorant display, Achilles and two other sock gremlins stared down the aisle to where a pair of guards waved flashlights back and forth.

Achilles smacked Shin-Splint across the back of his head. The young gremlin's smaller ear flattened, and his larger ear wobbled from the blow.

"You said there was only one guard," snapped Achilles.

Shin-Splint shrunk back and adjusted his ski mask. His mismatched eyes stared in opposite directions as he tried to count on his claws. "You know I have trouble with non-prime numbers. It's genetic. Besides, there's still more of us than them."

"There's two more by the doors." Bunion leaned between his co-conspirators and nodded across the aisle toward the front window.

Achilles followed the senior gremlin's gaze and saw two mannequins sitting in facing chairs with their pant legs pulled back to reveal Triceratops patterned socks. Achilles recognized the Jurassic Feet collection that had caught his attention earlier that day and inspired the sock caper.

He groaned, and the two guards stiffened.

"It's a pair of dummies," he hissed. "Where's your glasses, Bunion?"

Bunion patted down an oversized vest full of pockets that stretched from his shoulders to his feet. He retrieved several pairs of glasses and stacked them on his crooked nose, then tilted his head back for a better look.

"Oops. My bad," he said too loudly.

The guards turned toward the noise. One reached for his baton. The other grabbed a radio. He thumbed a button on its side, and a squawk resounded.

"A bunch of motion detectors have gone off," the guard said. "Joe and I are investigating. We think it might be raccoons. Did Mort fix that hole in the roof over the storage room?"

The radio mumbled.

"Well, Joe and I aren't animal control," the guard responded.

Achilles hauled his comrades deeper into the shadows. He'd come too far to turn back now. He'd lived too long on the meager subsistence of a toddler's forgotten ankle sock at the park or the frayed ends of a gold-toed dress sock left in the laundromat dryer. This store was full of socks, ripe for the eating, and all he had to do was fill a shopping cart and escape without being seen.

The sock gremlin code valued secrecy above all else. To be discovered by humans meant exile at best and execution by rubber bands at worst. Achilles cringed at the thought of a mob of sock gremlins surrounding him with thick elastic bands. Surely, nothing was worse than death by a thousand snaps.

"We should leave," whined Shin-Splint. "It's not worth the risk."

Bunion slapped a tiny souvenir hockey stick against his hand. "Naw, I got this. I'll sneak up behind them. They'll never see it coming."

He was facing the wrong direction. His glasses had slipped off his nose.

Achilles clenched his jaw so tightly a tooth cracked. His stomach growled. This was the caper of a lifetime, and these two were the best sock gremlins he could find on short notice. He would've pulled the job himself, but it took at least two gremlins to push a full shopping cart and one more to open the doors. Sock gremlins were fast and sneaky, but they were also quite small.

The guards stepped between racks of socks, and their flashlight beams narrowly missed the three would-be thieves. Achilles racked his brain for a plan, but he couldn't think on an empty stomach. Reaching up, he found Sockamoles, an avocado-themed running sock. He chowed down.

As he digested the cilantro-infused, buttery goodness, he considered the narrow aisles with their tall shelves of bestsellers like the Bacon-My-Heart, One-in-a-Melons, and Tea-riffics. How did such flimsy shelving hold such a wonderful buffet of socks?

The guards were only a few feet away now. Achilles grabbed Bunion by the shoulders and aimed him toward the two men. "Okay, champ. Go get them."

With a growl, Bunion charged forward and swung the stick. He caught the edge of a rack of Pugs-And-Kisses compression socks. The rack toppled, clocking one guard in the noggin. He dropped quicker than a pair of athletic socks filled with nickels.

"You okay, Joe?" The remaining guard gulped as he glanced nervously toward the ceiling tiles. When he leaned over his fallen coworker, Bunion scurried up his back and bit his ear. The guard jerked backward, flinging Bunion into a stack of Jamaican-Me-Crazy mid-calf socks.

Achilles shoved Shin-Splint away from the remaining guard. "Go! Grab as many socks as you can carry. I'm getting a cart."

Shin-Splint knocked over a cardboard cutout of Gwendolyn

Twinkletoe, the celebrity spokesperson of the Footsie Roll franchise, and one of his clawed feet punched through her illustrious smile. He hopped down the aisle. Stuck to his ankle, the cutout bumped behind him, dislodging thermal socks, knee highs, and loafers.

A flashlight beam sliced wildly through the air and landed on the retreating gremlin.

"Holy moley!" The guard choked his radio. "We've got a raccoon infestation! Call the county! Send animal control! Send the national guard! Just send help quick!"

Bunion shook free of an avalanche of Jamaican-Me-Crazies, let loose his war cry, and sprinted toward the hysterical voice while swinging at every shadow. The sock tornado careened toward the guard, who dropped his flashlight and ran for the nearest door.

"You're on your own, Joe!" he shouted over his shoulder. "I've got a wife and kids."

Grunting, Achilles rolled a cart toward Shin-Splint, who had finally freed his toes from Gwendolyn Twinkletoe. Bunion rejoined them with his splintered hockey stick.

The older gremlin panted. "Did it work? Did we get them?"

Achilles held up a pair of Tyrannosockus crew socks from the Jurassic Feet collection and grinned. "The sock buffet is open."

Shin-Splint shuddered. "Do you really think they have raccoons? I hear those critters have rabies."

Achilles vowed to find better help next time.

THE MENDER OF BROKEN THINGS

Emily Barnett

Bramble Dinkenspry was very good at fixing things. In fact, her entire family was good at it. But when you're a brownie, you expect nothing less.

"Bram! It's time!"

Bramble nearly dropped the stopwatch in her nimble fingers. She'd been listening to the gears as they whispered secrets of the device's inner workings. It was the uncanny Sense of her hobgoblin clan.

Bram left the room and joined her family in front of the blue door. Though brownies were no taller—and barely wider—than a pencil, they still had to be careful not to be seen by humans. Their job was simple: steal into the house at night, fix anything broken, and slip back into the wall. Although *wall* was a casual term. Brownies lived between the human and the hobgoblin world. Unlike fairies or selkies, brownies relied on fixing human objects to maintain their magic.

When her mother opened the door, wavering light and nausea rolled over Bram. The clan crept through and entered the human house by way of a spice cabinet. *At least it's not the freezer this time*, Bramble thought.

The five brownies clambered down the counter, swift as shadows. Bram's parents started on a light bulb. Her sister tiptoed to the bathroom's leaky faucet. Scratching his pointed chin, Bram's little brother studied a crack in the plaster wall.

Bramble headed up the stairs to the daughter's room.

She touched her thundering chest and the scrap of fabric she wore as a dress. Bram wasn't nervous about going into Cecily's room, but she *was* nervous about the parents.

Unbeknownst to the clan, Bram's Sense was... peculiar. She could hear the human realm from the hobgoblin side as easily as listening to a stopwatch's gears.

And what Bramble had heard the past few months had made her brave—or foolish—depending on which hobgoblin you asked. Imps, in particular, were always slandering the brownie's philanthropic ways.

Bram ran through the door and scrambled to Cecily's bedside table. A night-light cast the room in a blue haze. Bram smiled at the girl's round cheeks and curls; she looked so peaceful.

Cecily whimpered.

Bramble reached out but chided herself. Fixing broken objects gave brownies power, but *touching* a human drained them. It was why she hadn't told the clan anything. If they knew of her strong Sense and curiosity, they'd ban her from visiting humans.

But the risk was worth it to Bram. When she helped others, she was whole.

Scanning the room, Bram spied a doll with missing arms. She hopped to the toy then listened for the rest of it. Whispers came from the closet, and Bram found the arms inside, buried under a mound of clothes as if the girl was ashamed of what she'd done.

Bram repaired the arms, replaced missing hair, and sewed a ripped sleeve with gold thread. The glass eyes were dull, so she rubbed a thumb over them until they sparkled. *There*, Bram thought, *now she seems to be laughing.* Bram placed it in Cecily's arms and slipped back into her realm by way of a dresser drawer.

Bramble visited the girl many times that month—especially the nights she knew would be the hardest. When harsh voices arose and doors slammed. When Cecily's parents screamed rather than consoled. The power in human speech rivaled the strength of magic, and it always shook Bram to the core. But worse, she *saw* their effects on the girl, how they changed and molded her. The brownie used to be able to hear Cecily's laughter ringing into her realm. But Cecily's joy had grown quiet over the months while her night whimpering worsened.

How could she fix the child's inner workings? Bram sighed. When it came to human hearts, her magic did not whisper the remedy.

Three weeks later, Bram found a necklace on the stand and set about fixing the broken chain.

"Are you an angel?"

Bram stiffened. Her gaze turned to the little girl who was *supposed* to be asleep. Bram crouched low and considered running. But Cecily's brown eyes were wide with hope, causing Bram to relax. She wouldn't be the cause of another disappointment in Cecily's already sad life.

"Not an angel," Bram said. "I just fix things."

Cecily sat up and rubbed her eyes. Her hair was a tumbled mess. "Are you a fairy?"

Bram snorted. Fairies were the silliest of hobgoblins—and quite useless to humans. "No. I'm a brownie."

Cecily's expression wrinkled in confusion.

"Not the kind you eat," Bram clarified.

"You're the one who fixed Dolly." She held up the toy she'd been cradling. Bram was glad to see the arms still intact.

"Yes."

Cecily smiled, but it grew stale. "I broke her. I don't know why."

Bram finished fixing the locket then placed it on the nightstand. Taking a deep breath, she studied the girl. "I think..." She scrunched up her mouth. "...when people hurt deep inside, they want to let it out somehow. To feel better."

"Like when Mommy and Daddy fight?"

"Yes." Bram chewed her lip. "But it never truly feels better when that hurt is left on its own, does it?"

Cecily shook her head slowly. Then she perked up, a curl slipping into her eyes.

"Can *you* fix Mommy and Daddy?"

Bramble's throat constricted, and she looked away. "I'm sorry. I only repair objects."

"I thought so." Cecily slid back under her covers and stared up at Bram. She was still smiling. "Will you come back tomorrow night?"

Then, Bramble did something even braver than being seen.

The brownie jumped lightly onto the girl's pillow and planted a wisp of a kiss on her forehead. Bram felt a bit of magic leave her, but it was worth it.

"I'll watch over you every night, if you'd like."

Cecily nodded then closed her eyes.

As Bram watched over her, the girl did not whimper once.

Perhaps, the brownie thought, *this is how I can mend what is broken.*

THE DUAL DRAGON DILEMMA

J. L. Ender

Birdsong twittered through the forest. I raised my bow, a sick twinge in my gut. The time had come. After years of hunting, my search could end here. I pulled back the string, arrow already nocked. Crouching in the midst of a large bush, broad, green leaves brushed my tunic and my cheek.

The silver dragonling in the meadow snuffled and took another chomp from the enormous elk he had taken down. A hair bigger than an ox, his scales glittered in the sunlight.

I took a deep breath and let the arrow fly. With a gentle *thwap* it zipped toward its target fast as deadly thought.

The arrow sunk into the dragonling's chest, the barbed point drilling through scales into meat and viscera to slam into the young dragon's heart. A gush of fire burst from his jaws—and the wound—and it dropped, neck extended, wings out. Its body twitched a few times, then stilled.

I ran to the corpse. Now the real action would begin.

First, I retrieved my arrow. The shaft had snapped and the fletching was singed off, but the head was still good. Well, it would be after I cleaned off the sizzling blood.

I used the arrowhead to carve a circle in the dirt and grass around the dragon, then poured salt into the divot. This done, I started drawing the appropriate runes with a thick piece of chalk. Yes, chalk. Yes, it took a while.

Once the runes were drawn into the not-so-obliging earth, I took a tiny drop of my blood and flicked it into the newly made ring. The salt glowed a soft pink. I put a hand to the circle and forced my will into it.

A much larger dragon appeared standing above me. *Right* above me. His scales—silver with long streaks of blue at the temples and down its chest—blotted out canopy and sun and sky. I drew another arrow and nocked it, this one enchanted with powerful, deadly magic, but didn't raise it yet.

My heart hammered. *Why am I doing this? What could possibly be worth it? Nothing, that's what.*

"Who's there?" the dragon growled in a voice like a foghorn. "Who dared summon me?" The booming words sent birds squawking and cawing into the sky.

I cleared my throat and smiled broadly. "That would be me. Hello there. The name's Rolen. Rolen Oakenheel. Do you know anything about planar travel?"

"About what?" he snarled, head darting around. "Where the devil are you?"

"The multiverse?" I cleared my throat. "I'm looking for means to travel off-world."

"I might, I might indeed, but I'm not telling you, mystery voice!" He backed up a step, turning a tree behind him to splinters with a mighty crack. Serpentine eyes glared down first at me, then at the dragon I'd killed.

Oh, that's not good.

"Is that Gatahrast? Did you kill one of my spawn, then use him to summon me? That's awfully cold, even for an elf."

My smile faltered. "Well, yes. I did. He was terrorizing the local populace. Seemed like a good two for one, yes?" *And I was hoping you wouldn't see him...*

"Bring him back to life with your foul elvish witchcraft and I'll tell you whatever you want."

I coughed. "That might be... Well, that's outside my current skillset." *For now.* I made a mental note to research resurrection magicka. Could be useful, right?

"Then you'd better reverse this summoning," the dragon growled in a low rumble. "Or I'll turn you inside out looking for some good magics in your cold intestines."

I forced my smile back into place. "That's a charming offer, I assure you, but I can't do that either."

Time to cut my losses before I wind up very dead.

I fired the arrow. It plinked off one of the dragon's thick blue chest scales and turned a nearby tree to dust.

Whoops.

"Was that an enchanted arrow?" The dragon's gruff laughter boomed through the forest, making more birds—apparently with a weaker sense of self-preservation than the first group—take flight. "No arrow can pierce my hide!"

I need a plan B. What's my plan B?

But that had *been* my plan B. I had no other tricks up my sleeve. *Time to flee.*

The dragonling in the circle gasped and sat up.

I shrieked and fell to my behind, scuttling backward across the grass. "What in the seven hells?"

Steam hissed from his mouth and his wound. He blinked at me with bleary eyes.

So... not dead, apparently.

"He shot one of my hearts, Da," Gatahrast whined. After the foghorn bellow of the adult, this little one's deep voice seemed nasally in comparison.

The big dragon snorted, smoke rings puffing from both nostrils.

"Well, that's what you get for terrorizing the countryside, you little snit. Apologize to the villagers, and we'll be on our way."

"But Da..." The dragonling drew up its legs and hunched its back, sulking.

Still on the ground, I swallowed. "Well, all's well that ends well, right?"

"You are one lucky elf." The adult snorted again. "Lucky that I'm bored with killing your kind. Off with you."

I winced. "Um, planar travel?" I managed to force the words out, fighting past my own self-preservation instincts.

"You can find the ghost glass of Marin on the Tortan continent, in a cave high up in the mountains of Drunia."

"Okay, okay." I pulled out a sketchbook and started scribbling. "Which mountain?"

The dragon laughed. "You'll know it."

"Ghost glass... So I'm asking a ghost for information? Or the ghost glass will let me travel to other worlds?"

The dragon laughed again, and with that the two flapped off.

I stared at the scattered circle, the giant footprints, the drifting dust that had once been a young oak. I dusted off my hands and beamed. "That went rather well."

X

A DYING PHOENIX

READERS' CHOICE AWARD WINNER
Karyne Norton

Lyric's quill scratched across his parchment faster than the other mages-in-training, but he was still too slow to keep up with their bestiary professor.

The old man's robes dragged through phoenix droppings inside the hatchery. He smiled as they reached the nesting trees in the heart of the habitat, where at least a hundred phoenixes sat on their eggs.

"It's a little-known fact that not all phoenixes are reborn." Professor Dillbridge clucked his tongue and held out a shaky hand to the bird. His tremors had gotten worse this year, and he'd yet to take on an apprentice. "One in four lacks the attribute for rebirth."

The phoenix spread her wings, their span matching Lyric's lanky height. Her feathers flashed ruby and bronze with flecks of pale yellow, like the witch hazel petals they'd ground up in the apothecary. She nudged the professor with her burnished ochre beak.

Lyric stepped closer to the nearest brooding mother, tucking his quill and parchment in his robe pocket. He couldn't tear his gaze from the phoenix's scarlet eyes. "Is there a way to tell which ones will return?"

Professor Dillbridge stepped back as the phoenix stirred. "It looks like you're about to find out. Keep your distance."

The phoenix nudged the deceptively plain egg. A hairline fracture graced its surface, the shell finally chipping when the tiniest beak broke through.

A chorus of admiration broke out. Professor Dillbridge chuckled as a sticky peach ball emerged, angling blindly toward its mother.

Something in Lyric warmed, like he'd returned from school and his mother's bread had just come out of the oven. He rubbed at his chest, relishing the strange sensation.

The mother squawked and sat on her baby, startling several of the onlookers.

"Wait for it," Professor Dillbridge murmured.

Flames shot out from the nest, engulfing both mother and chick. Cries of dismay filled the hatchery before shifting to wonder.

Lyric's chest turned cold.

Professor Dillbridge stepped closer as the flames died down. "When a phoenix is born, the mother must test if the nestling will be reborn." He pulled on thick gloves, then dug through the ashes before pulling out a single pale pink chick. But no peach ball.

Only the mother had returned.

"She killed her own baby?" Lyric's throat grew tight, his voice pained.

"She tested it," Professor Dillbridge corrected, but his eyes held sadness. "It's the way of nature."

He passed the nestling off to a senior student headed for the artificial hatchery when another phoenix roused in her nest.

"Looks like we get to try our hand again." Professor Dillbridge beckoned them all over.

Lyric lagged behind, his heart heavy.

This time, a fuchsia nestling broke free from its egg, squawking as if it knew its fate. The warmth returned to Lyric's chest, but this time the heat made him double over. Fire rolled through his torso in waves, and his focus wavered until the phoenix burst into flames.

"Are you all right?" Professor Dillbridge placed a hand under Lyric's elbow.

The fire in Lyric's chest dissipated along with the flames in the nest. "Yes, I—I just got dizzy," he mumbled.

Professor Dillbridge eyed him suspiciously, then retrieved two nestlings from the ashes. The students cheered, but Lyric stayed quiet, his gaze straying to the first empty nest.

"Come," Professor Dillbridge said. "This next nest holds several eggs, most of them abandoned by mothers forced to go through their rebirth early."

As the others continued, Lyric stepped up to the first nest, running a finger through the warm ashes. Fluttering heat coursed through him again. The warmth of a single precious life. He soon rejoined the others, his heart no longer in the lesson.

Professor Dillbridge moved aside a brooding phoenix, ignoring her pecking, and revealed six eggs. "Feel how warm they are?"

The students placed palms on eggs. Lyric hesitated, then tentatively let the tips of his fingers graze the hard shell of the one nearest him. The same sense of home flooded him, and he relaxed against the egg. He let his hand graze a second one, but gasped as fire engulfed his chest. He pulled his hand back as though burned. Carefully, he tested the other eggs, feeling for warmth versus fire.

Only the second egg held the heat of infinite lifetimes.

"This is the only phoenix that will be reborn." Lyric winced as he touched the egg.

Classmates tittered, but Professor Dillbridge's gaze sharpened as he let the phoenix return to her eggs.

Lyric hesitated. "Can't you feel it?"

"Class dismissed," Professor Dillbridge said. "Lyric, stay with me."

The students whispered and lingered, while Professor Dillbridge led Lyric to a secluded fourth nest where another mother moved aside to let her baby hatch.

"Tell me," Professor Dillbridge whispered. "Which is it?"

A light amber bird emerged, and Lyric sensed hot chocolate and winter blankets. His heart sank.

Something in him snapped. He bolted forward as the mother phoenix squatted over her baby.

"No!" Lyric ignored his professor's warnings, reaching beneath the phoenix and fumbling for something soft and fragile. He hissed when the beak pricked his fingertip, but he wrapped his hand around the baby, pulling it to safety as the mother erupted in flames.

Lyric fell back, blocking his eyes and tucking the bird inside his robes.

"What were you thinking?" Professor Dillbridge bent over Lyric, eyes wide as he checked for injuries.

"This one won't be reborn." Lyric pulled the tiny nestling out from under his robes. The bird leaned into his hand. "He only has one life to live."

The professor straightened, face slack.

"He deserves to live it," Lyric mumbled. Would he receive demerits? Be sent home for his reckless behavior?

Professor Dillbridge's eyes glistened, his voice harsh. "In sixty years, only four students have had the gift, but you..." His gaze held wonder. "You're the first to save a dying phoenix."

He helped Lyric to his feet.

"Come. Today you start training as my apprentice."

SPHINX INDUSTRIES

Abigail Falanga

"We here at Sphinx Industries pride ourselves on ensuring that your property and information are secure..."

The pleasant voice of the promotional video drones on for the forty-seventh time—slight exaggeration—since I got here two hours ago. Long enough so that everyone has forgotten I'm here. I'm the kind of person people forget—slim young guy in a nice hoodie, probably delivering something. I'm virtually invisible. One of my more mundane talents.

Past closing time now, the last employees have left the large, modern building, security guards have done the night shift walkthrough, locked doors, and left one in position behind a front desk—and I'm still here. Halfway behind a pillar standing near the TV with the overproduced promo.

At least the ad is easy to ignore. The voice that hisses through my earbuds, not so much.

"It's time." My employer's voice is stiff and nagging. "Are you in position?"

"Have been for the last hour. Quit worrying," I mutter.

"Not worried. Just want it to go off without a hitch. You know why we brought you in, right?"

"'Cause I'm the best." I grin, though he can't see me.

"Yes," he confirms, a little too quickly. "You might succeed where all the others have failed."

This part of the job has never sat well with me. *All* the others? "Might help if you could pass on what they learned."

The boss doesn't answer—again—instead saying, "You have five minutes. Going dark *now*."

The electricity, phones, internet, everything shuts down. My mind shifts back to my task. The guard at the desk jumps to his feet and frantically tries to get his system to respond, yelling at his coworker through an unresponsive earpiece. I'm free to move through the shadowy lobby, up the stairs, toward the vaults on the third floor.

Sphinx Industries is the best security firm in the world, so they have backups for power outages. But I'm ready. Hacking is my thing, augmented by a knack for understanding the nuances of technology—not that I tell anyone much about that part. It takes me twenty seconds to manipulate the door's complex locks, first entering a code of my own devising and then tripping a wire, and I'm through into the vast server vault.

I slip into the blue twilight of the gigantic chamber and start toward the server that's my goal. It'll take me another minute to find and secure the drive, assuming I don't encounter more security measures.

"Stop, intruder," a deep voice purrs from somewhere above.

Like this one, apparently.

AI security system? This must be the advanced tech SI advertised—and what stopped my predecessors.

I advance another cautious step, waiting to see what it'll do and brainstorming how to respond.

"No farther." The voice is so close I imagine the hint of a breath.

Next instant, I stagger backward. A huge paw steps out of the shadows, followed by a massive catlike body—a *winged* one. It towers over me, beautiful, solid, otherworldly.

Dangerous.

"I do not know you." It bares sharp teeth.

"What are you?" I gasp.

"A sphinx, obviously—the great secret at the heart of this firm's success," it replies smugly. "Have you the password, stranger?"

"But… sphinx are myths!"

It bends its head to sniff me. "You ought to believe in myths, with magic like *that* in your veins. Or do you know nothing more than how to manipulate computer code?"

"Hey, I know things!" I blurt, trying to recall anything I've ever half-heard about sphinxes, hoping I can back up the boast. "You do the riddle game, right? If I can answer three riddles correctly, you have to let me get what I want."

"Sounds more entertaining than passwords." The sphinx tilts its head, then lies down just in front of me, tail twitching across its legs and wings. "Very well, wizard. Answer three questions correctly and take what you want. Fail to answer, and I shall eat you like I did the others."

Fear stabs through me. "I don't have much choice, do I? You'll eat me if I run."

"Then don't run. First question: What do tyrants seek yet lies behind every wall socket?"

"Easy! Power."

"Easy, was it?" The sphinx's chuckle is anything but reassuring. "Second question: Why are you here?"

Not so easy. If I answer the truth—that I'm supposed to steal something entrusted to the security-sphinx—I'm in trouble. I start to reply. "I was hired to retrieve something…"

"Why?"

"I never ask. They want. I provide. Was that the third question?"

"Same question, because you are taking so long to answer it. Again—*why you?*"

"'Cause I'm the best."

"Are you?" Sharp claws tap on the tiled floor but don't approach. The sphinx is leading me to the answer.

Which is that I'm not the best. Far from it. I'm competent, but I have no credentials and very little reputation. "They hired me because I'm a nobody who'll get the job done." I speak the truth even as I realize it. "I'm expendable."

The sphinx blinks once—a smile in cat language. "Third question: What fate awaits all, but which all avoid?"

A shiver runs through me as I open my mouth. No words come.

"A hint." It lowers its head until wide golden eyes are level with mine. "This fate awaits you whether you succeed or fail, whether truth or self-deception comes from your lips, whether you leave this room or I devour you."

"Death," I barely whisper.

"You have answered correctly." The sphinx rises and pads to one side. "Take what you wish."

I stumble to the server, find what I've been sent for, then turn, drive in hand. "They're gonna kill me, aren't they?"

"That's your concern now. I like you, Wizard, so I gave you every warning I could." It gives itself a shake and stretches its wings. "Thank you for doing business with Sphinx Industries."

PRAIRIE DRAGON

S. M. Jake

"Daggum scientists!" Penny growled. Hefting her skirts higher, she tore through the brome toward a cluster of cottonwoods. A raspy roar echoed across the open plain, and she glared back at said scientist. "You just had to poke the prairie dragon!"

"Actually, dragon is a misnomer," Benjamin huffed, struggling to keep up. He glanced yet again over his shoulder, that stupid boyish grin growing lopsided. "This would be *Pterodactylous nebraskaneous*. A descendant of *Pterodactylous antiquus*."

Wings beat behind them, and Penny grabbed his arm, jerking him to move faster. *Why* did she keep accepting these jobs? Sure, East Coasters had a fascination with the Wild West and money to spend on it—the scientific crowd especially. Show 'em a bunch of layers in a rock, dig up a few wildflowers to watch the magic veins spark, point out a hustlin' jackalope, or take 'em up a hill to look over grazing buffalo herds or sleeping prairie dragons, and they bubbled with excitement. But this guy? He was turning out to be a new depth of East Coaster trouble! Awkward and academic, perpetually curious, with a contagious enthusiasm that bubbled up over the most simple things. And the most deadly.

Sparks hit the ground. Hot saliva splattered her hem and

boots, and a shadow swept overhead.

Penny yanked Benjamin into the meager tree cover, hopped down the shallow bank, and ducked behind a hefty cottonwood trunk. He missed the hop and fell, sprawling into the thick mud of the not-quite-dry creek bed. Penny cringed. All week, he had regaled her with tidbits and scientific facts: many delightful, some superfluous. But, in this moment, it bordered on infuriating.

"Benjamin, that ain't a dinosaur!" She hated using his first name. It wasn't professional. But she couldn't manage the mouthful of his last name with her heart thundering like a runaway mule.

He pushed up onto his feet, tacky mud caking his chin and chest, eyes bright as he skimmed the canopy for the beast. "Not exactly, no. It's related to the pterodactyl, which by definition isn't a dinosaur, but of the Pterosauria order, to—"

A roar cut across the prairie, making the tree quiver against her back.

"If it looks like a dragon, and it sounds like a dragon"—Penny jerked her Colt from her pocket, a shower of sparks and coals falling through the canopy twenty feet from them—"and it spews fire like a dragon, it's a dragon!"

She double-checked the pocket revolver.

"You can't shoot it!" Benjamin stretched out toward her, fighting to free his feet from the mud. "They're a symbol of the Great American West! A scientific marvel within the zoological world!"

"Like it'll even feel a .31." She fought an eye roll, watching for the tell-tale shadow. "I'll be lucky if I can annoy it into leaving us alone."

"But, if it leaves…" Benjamin finally dragged himself out of the muck, stumbling into the trunk beside her. "When will we ever get such an amazing first-hand experience? I mean, people back home dream of such marvels."

Penny's nose wrinkled at the scent of dirt and sweat clinging to him. Or maybe it was his absurd fascination with things that could kill them.

"Just watch," he whispered. He reached around her, pointing out the dark shadow as it came out of the sun. "The way it moves, it's completely unlike a bird or bat. The aerodynamics play so differently. And here, when it tips just so..."

The prairie dragon banked, light catching on its scales, flashes of blue and green and brown easing across the sky in a way that wasn't exactly graceful, but flowing, strength radiating from each beat of its wings.

Penny's breath caught. She'd lived near these critters all her life, growing up surrounded by the rugged charm of Nebraska Territory. How had she stopped noticing? When did she grow indifferent to this beauty? And how was it this city boy saw more wonder in the wilds than she did?

The dragon doubled back, and Benjamin shifted, unconsciously moving closer to her. She barely turned, watching the wonder and delight spill out across his face. Wide eyes, same blue as the open sky. Straw-blond hair tumbling across his forehead. The line of his jaw that much better with a bit of dirt on it. Something sparked in Penny's chest, building as he smiled absentmindedly, stoking heat into her cheeks.

His gaze shifted, locking onto hers.

Penny's face burned, and she threw her elbow into his ribs.

Benjamin stumbled backward with a wheeze, one foot squishing into the mud. "What was that for?"

She spun, fighting not to fan her flaming face, and spotted the dragon drifting lazily into the distance. She triple-checked her Colt anyway. "Daggum scientists."

SHENANIGANS

Deborah Bainbridge

I can't believe I landed my red breeches in detention again.

"Dia dhuit!" Mrs. O'Grady, a plump fiery-haired lady, walks past a row of my classmates and removes my green top hat by its gold buckle. "Third time this year, isn't it, Skylar? You're seventeen and as mischievous as the next leprechaun. Haven't you learned how to avoid this by now?" She taps my boots, a reminder to remove them from the seat in front of me. "What sort of trouble brings you here today?"

I grin and stroke my red chinstrap beard. "During recess, my little brother and I fetched water from the stream in Carlingford Cavern. I told ím a sheepdog was headed straight for us. He shot down into the cave like a shrieking banshee was after ím."

"That poor, wee lad. I bet you frightened the shamrocks out of ím! I'm surprised you didn't say it *was* a banshee."

"Good idea, Mrs. O'Grady. I'll use that one next time."

My classmates snicker.

Mrs. O'Grady adjusts her red spectacles and throws me a stern look. "You excel at hiding gold to fool humans, but we never prank fellow leprechauns. They won't trust us again."

"You've been saying that for years, but I've fooled Rowan loads of times. Leprechauns are tricksters! I'm just improving my craft."

"Rowan's eleven. He may be naïve, but he's not stupid. Farmer O'Hare has several Atlantic Sheepdogs. Mark my words, Skylar"—she points her finger at me—"one day, your little brother won't believe you and you'll be wishing he had. Mind you keep those tattered black boots on a straight path."

She addresses the class. "Repeat the Leprechaun Rules after me. One, tell the truth to all leprechauns. Two, deceive any human or beast who poses a threat to our kin. Three, evade capture at all costs."

She opens a canister and the air fills with sweetness. The one good thing about detention: Mrs. O'Grady always sends us off with something sweet afterward.

I savor my cookie as I walk through the weathered cavern passageways. Our small cottage is located near the narrow opening to the fjord, Carlingford Lough. I tiptoe through the back door and nearly jump out of my boots when I see a short figure in a tartan dress watching me.

"Mam!" I clutch my vest. "Have I told you how that dress brings out the blue in your eyes?"

"As a matter of fact, you have."

"Dinner smells delicious! What are we having?"

"Roasted potatoes and cabbage." Mam's eyebrows arch. "I've told your brother never to trust you again. Go apologize. And feed your ladybird. You were almost late for dinner; she's hungry."

"One thing about me, Mam: I'm never late for dinner."

I rush to feed Scarlet, my seven-spot ladybird, but stop short at Rowan's bedroom door. He doesn't look up when I enter.

"Rowan?"

He traces the shamrocks on his quilt.

"Ah, come on, Rowan. It was just a bit of fun."

His red freckled face gets even redder. "You lied to me *again*, Skylar. I trusted you."

"Sorry. Sometimes I just can't resist a good prank."

Rowan scowls.

"Let's go feed Scarlet together, yeah?"

"All right." Rowan follows me outside reluctantly. "Someday, I want a ladybird that rides on my shoulder and delivers messages for me, too."

"Then, we best find one for you to bond with."

Rowan's face lights up with a beatific smile.

At sunrise, we journey to Farmer O'Hare's rose garden—an aphid buffet. Rowan stealthily approaches a beautiful ladybird resting on a pink, velvety rose. He rests a finger on the black spot that adjoins her wings and holds her gaze for three seconds. Her antennae click and the bond is complete. She lands on Rowan's shoulder and he beams with delight.

"I'll name her Rose."

"Spectacular!" I look past Rowan at a large, dark form in the field and freeze. Rowan glances up at me. Seeing terror on my face, he stills. "Run," I whisper urgently. In a flash, his little legs dash like lightning bolts toward home.

Trickster extraordinaire! I double over with laughter. When I rise, I notice the grass shift. The hair on my arms stands. The dark form across the field is missing. *Where did it go?* I gulp.

A low growl emanates. I can't breathe. Eyes peer through the grass and I dart toward the nearest tree. Scarlet latches onto my coat. She flutters her wings, attempting to help me climb. I hear a jaw snap as I lift my foot onto the branch. My throat closes as a howl reaches me from the base of the tree.

"Any idea where your brother is?" Mam asks Rowan. "Skylar's a prankster, for sure, but he's never been late for dinner. It's fifteen past."

Rowan glances up from his plate of roasted potatoes, the color draining from his face. "I thought it was another trick."

"You thought *what* was another trick?"

"Skylar sent Scarlet with a message saying he was treed by the farmer's sheepdog. Do you think he was actually telling the truth?"

"A dose of his own medicine may be just the thing to teach ím a hard lesson. But, no matter the shenanigans, he may need help." She tosses her apron onto the table. "Rowan, send Rose with an urgent message to Skylar. Tell ím I'm sounding the warning bell."

Loud chimes echo throughout Carlingford Cavern, calling the clan to action.

Considering my fate, a chunk of sap stuck to my pants is the least Mam will scold me for. Shaking as I clutch a tree limb, a potato catapults through the air above me. Then another. I spy my clan in the distance.

They're using the spud-launcher to lure the fur-beast away!

I thank my lucky clovers that I live in Ireland where even sheepdogs love potatoes. I climb down to embrace Mam and Rowan.

"I promise I will never be the leprechaun who cries sheepdog again."

A BROTHER'S LOVE

Andrew Hayes & Daniel Gomez

"C'mon slowpoke, hurry up. We're almost there," Shard called, scrambling ahead. Her claws trampled over the fallen pines.

"Would you slow down?" Krag wheezed. His crooked wing trailed behind him like a torn sail. Why did she always have to rush ahead? As her older brother, shouldn't he be leading her?

They emerged from the frosty woods. Shard gasped, "Oh, look."

The majestic mountain range pierced an overcast sky through billowing gray cotton clouds. Like everything else in this frozen world, a blanket of snow cloaked the jagged peaks. Before the siblings, the cliff broke off several dragon-lengths away—the last sight before the endless expanse of thick dark fog.

"I never agreed to come here," Krag complained, wincing at his broken wing, its platinum gray scales deformed by small holes.

"Wow," Shard started again, "you can really see the drop from here."

At that moment, he watched as her stout legs took off once more, barreling ever faster toward the cliff. At the last second, Shard spread her little wings to slow herself and skidded to a stop, teetering just past the bluff.

Krag pulled up behind her. "Would you please not do that?"

She giggled, "Oh, that's right. Of all the creatures on this tundra, I had to get the scaredy brother who couldn't fly. You're supposed to be stronger and braver. You're not being a very good older brother."

It was true. Ever since the accident which left his wing warped, Krag wasn't much of an adventurer.

Glancing down, Krag muttered, "Look, you're too young to fly, and well, I can't. I know you said you've been here before, but that was with Dad. Let's be a little safer since he's not here; back up."

"What, back up? No way. You can really feel the breeze with your scales out like this, try it."

"Shard, please."

The little dragon danced about, laughing and sticking one leg over the edge.

"Hey, it's not funny, Shard. Back up."

"Just lighten up. Have a bit of fun. It's not even dangerous." She stomped the ground. "This cliff is just something the parents squawk about. It's not gonna—"

The sheet gave out, and the young hatchling dropped out of sight.

"Shard!" Krag craned his neck over the side, horrified of what he would see.

Maniacal laughter spat in his face.

About twenty feet below, his brat of a sister lay sprawled out on a smaller ledge, tousled, but safe.

"My gosh, your face, it's priceless." Shard squealed, rolling around in a fit of hysteria. "Now help me up."

With a sigh of annoyance and relief, Krag kneeled and stretched out his rugged arm.

"It won't reach, Popsicle-head. Climb down and get me."

Krag never appreciated when his sister bossed him around. He was older, but she always knew how to exploit his love and use her vulnerability to get what she wanted.

But she was safe. He just had to grab her and carry her back up. Then they would go home. He wouldn't roll the dice again.

Krag clambered down, dropping next to his sister.

"Took you long enough." Shard smirked. "Do you think if I jump and spread my wings, I could glide over to that other side?"

Suddenly, the ledge splintered from the shelf, and the two plummeted into the dismal void.

Krag's stomach lurched into his throat. The frigid air whipped around him, muffling his screams.

"Krag, help!" a distant cry wailed.

Krag had to do something. But what?

The wind whistled through his punctured wing, a grim reminder of his inadequacy. He sunk his sharp talons into the cliff face, but they barely scratched the wall. He tried freezing his claws onto the rock with his icy breath, but his tumble through the mist was too violent, and the ice shattered.

"Krag!"

He panicked as he saw the labyrinth of jagged rocks and unending frozen spikes at the bottom of the bluff. He and his sister were going to become dragon shish kebabs. He had no other choice; he could not let his sister die.

His heart froze, and his fear vanished with a newfound surge of power. A cold frost spread from his heart throughout his whole body, hardening his scales and turning them pure white. The cold spread to his wings, encapsulating his wounds with a frigid membrane that shimmered like a freshly-formed icicle. His claws gained jagged edges, and a strange, blue crystalline hue covered his eyes.

He spread his dazzling, ice-glazed wings and roared like an

avalanche. He glanced to his left—his wounds now sealed by the edged ice—the whistling ceased, and he found himself aloft, rising, beating his wings through the chilly air.

Krag plunged into the abyss, wings now tucked closely to his body. As he nosedived through the haze, he caught sight of a writhing silhouette frantically flapping, trying to keep herself aloft. He caught up with his sister and grasped her with all four talons. Spreading his wings, he strained to slow their descent, but their bodies still collided painfully with the frozen, unforgiving ground, barely missing a giant ice stalagmite.

"Krag, you flew. How did you do that?"

"I don't know. I was worried that you would die, and suddenly I felt super cold, and it healed my wounds, and I could fly."

She ran over and buried her tear-soaked face in his frosty shoulder.

"What was I thinking? I should have listened to you, then we fell, but you saved me, and…"

"And now you're safe, and that's what matters."

Krag embraced his little sister, determined to keep her safe for as long as he lived.

LEGENDARY LOCATIONS

LADY HOOD

Jenneth Leed

Ever since a wolf devoured Marian's grandmother, the Sheriff of Nottingham had set a permanent watch on his daughter, which made it rather difficult to sneak into the forest, but not impossible.

Marian huffed and pulled her red riding cloak tighter to ward off the morning chill. Her father hadn't been particularly fond of Grandmother Nottingham—he'd grind his teeth every time she criticized the way he twisted his mustache at the ends. She thought it made him look devilish, like those "ruffian thieves" in the wood.

Father did not appreciate being compared to ruffian thieves.

But the tragedy of Grandmother's death lit a fire under Father, and he feared that one day such a creature might come for *her* if she ever entered the wood alone.

"He's right, you know. The forest can be a dangerous place." Robin leaned casually on his longbow, a fox-like smirk playing on his lips. "I hear there are outlaws about."

The legendary Hood wore a simple green jerkin, stockings torn from the thistles, and a quiver over his shoulder. It was the way he always appeared, unless he was donning one of those ridiculous disguises he so loved.

Marian dredged up a half-baked smile and pressed her fingers into the fallen log beneath her. "Father's solution is to marry me off to some silly nobleman in the east, away from wolves and outlaws and adventure. Away from Sherwood." She frowned to keep the sudden tears at bay. "Away from *you*."

Robin twirled the longbow, one end digging a hole in the forest floor. "You can't be rid of me that easily, Mari."

"He's already found a suitor."

The longbow stopped mid-twirl, and Robin's face tightened. Though his words remained light, a stiffness pervaded his voice. "A stuffy nobleman worthy of Marian Nottingham? I find that unlikely."

Marian's fingers twisted in her cloak until she feared that the wool would tear. "He claims the title of best huntsman in the country and boasts that his bow skills are akin to none."

Robin sniffed. "Again, I find that unlikely."

Marian rolled her eyes. "Honestly, Robin, he sounds as self-centered as you."

Robin recoiled, glaring. "*Highly* unlike—" He cleared his throat. "Who is this nobleman anyway? I should like to know the name of the man who claims to best me in my greatest attributes."

"We've not met him." Marian's shoulders slumped a little. "But my father's written to him many times... a 'Lord Goldfinch.' What an utterly ridiculous name for a nobleman."

Robin leaned his longbow against a tree and came to sit beside her. "I'm rather fond of it, actually."

Marian gave him a shove, nearly causing him to topple into the brook behind them. "My *wretched* Hood, you are not helping!" She denied the smile tugging at her lips. "I don't want to be a Lady *Goldfinch*. I want to be a Lady *Hood*."

"Then Lady Hood you shall be," he declared, righting himself. "I ought only to win the approval of the sheriff."

Marian eyed him. "You would have to relinquish thievery."

"Done."

"And kill a wolf."

"I slay wolves before breakfast."

Marian groaned. "Robin, *please...*" He was always going on about impossible feats, pretending to be someone he was not... Just once she wished he'd—

Robin took her hands in his calloused grip, a glimmer of something sober and determined ghosting his usually merry eyes. "Marian, I swear to you, I *will* win your father's favor. We *will* be together one day."

She tightened her fingers around his, wishing for his words to be true, but unsure how it could be possible. "But Goldfinch... He's already given a date for the wedding, and my father's favor lies solely with him."

"And you have no idea who he is?"

Marian shook her head.

Robin dropped her hands and stood, taking up his bow like he'd just accepted a quest. "Right, then. I'm looking for a huntsman with uncontested archery skills and an ego as large as a longbow. Considering I'm the only one who currently fits that description, this may prove difficult." He winked at her before vanishing into the forest. "I give you my word, Mari. You shall never suffer such a dismal name as *Goldfinch* as long as I live."

Robin Hood was an outlaw. A liar. A thief. But when Robin gave his word, Marian knew he would keep it on pain of death. She knew that somehow he would stop the wedding, and so she waited, plastering blithe smiles in view of her father, feigning excitement for the coming day.

Until her father brought home a broken longbow, mauled

apart by a wild beast.

"I'm sorry, my dear," he murmured, and Marian believed a very small part of him might have been telling the truth.

She cried herself to sleep as wolves howled from the forest.

....

Marian stood at the altar as the priest recited holy rites between her and... *Lord Goldfinch*. Marian repressed a shudder. The nobleman appeared even more absurd in person than she'd imagined: a twisted mustache that appeared to be deliberate mockery of her father's, caterpillar eyebrows, and he even had the nerve to cloak himself in a thick wolfskin—a trophy from his recent hunt.

Robin would have snapped an arrow at the sight.

"Do you take this woman to be your wife?" asked the priest.

"I do." Goldfinch gathered her hands in his oddly calloused grip, and she loathed how they reminded her of a certain foolhardy outlaw.

Wait... Marian squinted at the nobleman. Had she caught something fox-like in his eyes, just now?

He leaned forward, voice just a breath of a whisper. "Now that I think of it," he said, "'Goldfinch' really *is* an utterly ridiculous name." His caterpillar brows waggled. "Don't you agree... Mari?"

The priest was speaking, but Marian didn't hear a word. She stared into the man's eyes, past the facades, her heart rushing and bringing life into her bones.

"I do," she breathed.

FOUNTAIN AND FIRE

Kat Heckenbach

Melinda nudged Kalek in the ribs. "C'mon, this'll be fun. My parents brought me here when I was a kid. It's kinda cheesy, but it's entertaining."

They'd been standing in the ticket line for several minutes, and Kalek was already fidgety. Despite his calm Elven exterior, he thrummed with energy. Melinda had spent two weeks trying to convince him to visit St. Augustine, Florida. He'd finally agreed when she told him it was the location of the Fountain of Youth.

She'd waited until they'd arrived in the old city to tell him the fountain was just a tourist attraction.

"I have to disguise my heritage for a *ruse*?" he'd snarled. He hated hiding his ears. Hated even more the T-shirt she made him wear instead of his tunic. She'd allowed the leather pants and boots because he said he'd rather chop off his hair than put on a pair of jeans.

They reached the window, and Melinda purchased two tickets. As soon as they stepped through the entryway and into the courtyard, Kalek stopped and tightened his grip on Melinda's hand.

"What are those?"

"They're peacocks. Just... fancy birds. Don't worry, they're friendly enough."

In Kalek's homeland it was nothing to spy a dragon, but peacocks were the things of fairytales. "They look like over-preened blue phoenixes."

Kalek squinted at the cluster of peacocks, then his face relaxed and one eyebrow twitched upward. He began to hum softly.

The peacocks shuffled forward a few steps and ruffled their fanned tail feathers.

Feathers that now sparkled.

The average human would write it off as sunlight reflecting on the plumes, but Melinda's power enhanced her perception, allowing her to see the truth others could not: the peacocks had magic. It was faint, subtle, but unmistakable.

"You sense it, too?"

Kalek nodded, his long curls shifting and allowing his pointed ears to poke through. She reached up and covered them again.

"That is so freaking cool." She tugged his hand and stepped toward the entry to the building that housed the fountain itself.

Stone walls created a cave-like feel, despite the wooden ceiling. In the center of the open room was a structure that looked like a fireplace, but which held a pipe emitting streams of water.

Kalek's breath tickled Melinda's ear as he whispered, "This is the fount you dragged me here for?"

Melinda sighed. "Technically it's an underground spring. They have to pipe the water up." She let go of his hand, then grabbed two of the little paper cups stacked next to the fountain and filled them. "Here." She held a cup in front of him. "Just drink it."

Kalek took the cup, which looked even smaller in his long musician's fingers. He touched the water it contained with the pinky of his other hand, as though testing it for toxicity, while Melinda lifted her own cup to her lips.

His eyes widened.

She stopped her movement. "What?"

Without answering, Kalek stepped over and knelt in front of the fountain. Eyes closed, he passed his hand through one stream of water.

Melinda moved closer. "Seriously, what?"

He began to hum as he had for the peacocks, but then morphed the sounds into words from the ancient Elven language he often used in his songs.

Melinda's eyelids pulled shut as Kalek's singing, his magic, enveloped her. She would have reminded him about the tourists in the room, but the song held her tongue.

Images formed around Melinda, as clear as if her eyes were wide open—the building was replaced by wilderness untouched by humans. She recognized some of the Florida fauna, like saw palmetto and cypress trees. At her feet, water bubbled up directly from the limestone ground of the clearing—no pipes or pumps. How long ago was this?

A sound broke through Kalek's song: a bird's caw.

Branches rustled and swayed as though in response.

Then it appeared. High above the trees, circling, brighter than the daylight streaming through the opening in the canopy. It swirled and dove, closer and closer.

Melinda stepped back despite knowing the creature in the vision could not see her.

A whorl of red-and-yellow, it landed gracefully on the limestone ground.

A phoenix.

Its feathers gleamed as it guzzled the water greedily.

No—the feathers were bright, but something was off. The phoenix had bare patches on its skin, and it hunched over as if in pain. It was old, sick, dying.

It drank and drank, then finally lifted its head and spread its wings.

Burst into flame.

And in its place, a brilliant red egg.

The image played over and over, each time ending with the egg, but each egg veined with more and more blue.

Kalek's singing stopped, and Melinda opened her eyes. The tourists in the room were standing as if dazed. The magic would be nothing but a faint memory, not unless Kalek intended it to hold, so Melinda ignored them and gazed at him.

"Does that mean—" She couldn't finish the question, but Kalek nodded.

"The phoenix," he said. "It used the fountain's powers. But each use must have drained the magic, and over time..."

"Peacocks!" Melinda laughed. "Still, that means it was real. Ponce de León actually found the Fountain of Youth." She peered into the cup in her hand, then downed the water in one gulp.

Kalek sighed and turned his cup upside down above the fountain.

"Why did you do that?"

"The magic belongs here."

"I didn't think about that." Melinda crumpled the cup. "Do you think if they closed this place down, the magic would build back up?"

Kalek shrugged and put his arm around her. They walked out of the building and came face-to-face with a peacock, its brilliant blue tail fanned out. It shivered, then turned and strutted away. A single red feather lay where it had stood.

RYDINGER AND THE WOLF

Andrea Renae

Rydinger flipped the hood over his head as a chill wind whipped around a corner. He clutched the waxed fabric parcel closer.

"You sure about this, Red?" His insides twisted at his cowardice. Nessa deserved better.

The shadow in front of him didn't slow.

"I guess that's my answer," he muttered, quickening his pace to match the towering woman's stride.

"Get the Goods to Old Mother," she finally grunted after they'd passed under the last bar of manufactured green light. "Don't get caught. What else is there to be sure 'bout?"

Rydinger peered behind him. "What exactly am I smuggling?" The alley was empty, but that didn't mean anything. The Wolf could be anywhere.

Just think about your sister. Think about Nessa.

Red turned abruptly. Her wiry hair escaped in a haze from under her cap. "That ain't your business. Got it?" Her shrewd eyes landed on Rydinger, as if she could read his insecurities like computer code. But her gaze eased. "If the Wolf finds you, run. The rest is on you, kid." She jerked her head toward the yawning darkness. "Old Mother's waitin'. Now, *scat*."

Four steps into the shadows, Rydinger's confidence flatlined. "I'm not sure I'm ready..." He turned to the last Light District, but Red had already vanished.

Going through the Black Out Zone was the only option now.

Fumbling to hold the Goods, Rydinger dug inside his jacket. He pulled out a rattly torch and swore when it didn't click on. He smacked it a few times on his knee, sweat beading on his brow. A feeble beam shuddered into existence.

The Boz was a labyrinth of dead ends and dilapidated buildings. All the smugglers had been given a rough map to study. Very rough. Incomplete.

He gripped the electric torch. It was one thing to find something like it. Quite another that it still worked. His sister had chanced upon it years ago, but she was too young to know what it was or that having it was dangerous. Rydinger had quickly confiscated it.

Now, he was glad he had. With a light to guide the way, the Boz was just like any other district.

He stood straighter.

An hour into climbing through rubble and spooking at several blasted rats, the torch began to flicker.

"*No...* no, no, *no!*"

It went out.

Darkness swooped in. Rydinger gulped, trying to control his rampaging heart. Why couldn't he remember the map? Nessa had helped him go over it a dozen times. A hundred.

A clatter sliced through the pounding in his ears. He spun toward the sound. The Goods slipped out of his hand, rolling into the surrounding darkness.

The noise again.

"Who's there?"

Footsteps crunched in response. He felt for the cold metal of his pocket blade, flipped it open, and swung it around.

"Peace, child." The voice was feminine. "You'll hurt yourself."

Rydinger flushed but kept the knife raised. He honed in on the stranger's position. "You're the Wolf." He used the name as a weapon.

She sighed, and something heavy scraped against gravel. She must have found the Goods.

"Do you know what this is?"

"My ticket out of this hell," he spat.

A soft laugh brushed his senses. "And what if I told you the thing you're using to negotiate freedom is what ensures this city will remain a 'hell'?"

There was a slicing sound, and the Boz filled with impossible light. Rydinger struggled to make his eyes focus. A slight-framed woman wrapped in layers of gray came into view. Her hair was a shimmering cascade without pigment. Countless cares etched her face.

This tired, unassuming woman was the Wolf? The legend that put fear into every smuggler who entered the Boz?

Her street name did not suit her.

"You have a choice." She held out a glowing sphere and dropped the thick fabric that had concealed it. "Take this and work toward purchasing an escape..."

He eyed the orb hungrily. All the threats, all the secrecy surrounding the Goods finally made sense. "Or?"

"Or give it back to the ones who cannot leave."

The Wolf approached and gently pushed the blade aside.

One choice between freedom and the fate of a cursed city.

"What will you choose?"

Rydinger's eyes lost focus on the dazzling spectacle. It would only take a few orbs to earn his release, but how many more would he need to secure Nessa's? His sister was deteriorating rapidly from the Shadowblight that ravaged the poorer districts, where true light was scarce. And he had been about to hand over the very thing she needed most of all.

His efforts to save her could be the reason she would die.

The untruths and the guilt swirled so violently, he felt sick. But he grasped at one sure thing.

Old Mother was stealing light from the city—light sick kids needed to survive.

Hot anger cut through his immobilizing thoughts. He grabbed the sphere and hurled it against a wall. It shattered into a thousand luminescent fractals, and he threw out a hand to snag a shard before it could escape. His breath caught as he watched the rest float to the sky. That single orb already made an infinitesimal difference in the gloom. Maybe with enough of them released, light—*health*—would no longer be a privilege for the wealthy.

The woman's illuminated face spread with a smile before she faded into the Boz's oblivion.

Rydinger returned to the Light Districts, armed with truth that left no room for cowardice. He sheepishly reported another victory for the Wolf.

Red was furious, but she bought the lie.

When he returned home to his sister trapped in her Shadowblight sleep, he retrieved the shard from his pocket. The blinding thing burned in his palm. He raised a fist and let the Wolf's gift drift to the ceiling.

Nessa's eyes opened.

Rydinger would do everything in his power to ensure more victories would follow.

WAKING UGLY

Kez Sharrow

Waking to a kiss *sounds* romantic. I mean, I had no problem with the kiss itself—soft lips, tickle of a mustache, faint licorice flavor. But, oh my goodness, people, what was a *man* doing in my *bedroom*?!

I sat bolt upright. My forehead smacked against his.

Ouch.

He staggered back from my bed, holding his head.

Curly brown hair, tall frame. "*Chiswell?*" My betrothed had sneaked into my bedroom? Dad would have a fit. I snatched the bedspread to cover my nightdress and inhaled dust.

"Actually, I'm Phillip. Chiswell's my great—"

"Don't care how great a friend you are of Chiswell's." This Phillip was sort of cute in a slicked-back-hair, needed-a-shave-yesterday kind of way, and I felt bad about the red spot between his eyes, but still. "Do you know what guys who come into a girl's bedroom and kiss her while she's sleeping are called?"

"Heroes?"

"Stalkers." I sneezed.

"Bless you." Phillip wore a dazed expression, like someone who'd expected a kitten and gotten a fire-spitting dragon instead.

"Guards!" I yelled, flinging off the covers and snatching up my robe.

A long scrape sounded outside, then a muffled thud.

"I think they're—" Phillip stepped toward me.

"Don't come any closer!" I raised my hand.

Good grief, what happened to my fingernails? Overgrown, they curled like a storybook witch's. I stepped out of bed. Instead of fluffy slippers, my feet touched a thick pile of dusty straw. I stood and felt a tug on my scalp. Eek! That straw was my hair.

I took a step, but the weight of my hair yanked me back. I pulled forward. Dust rose from the coiled locks, but the hair itself didn't budge.

"I'm like that girl with the unfortunate name," I wailed. "Parsley? Radish?"

"Rapunzel?"

"That's the one." I strained forward, scalp burning. Ugh. The hair was winning.

"May I?" Phillip flipped a knife from his belt.

I jumped. He was armed!

"For the hair..."

"Oh, right." I took the knife and sawed at the hair. Mizzi would be horrified. Where was she, anyway? I scanned the room. The drapes were gray, the rugs a mottled brown, and everything on my dresser in dire need of scrubbing.

"How did you get in?" The door was obviously shut.

"Through the window."

"You couldn't possibly. The tower's half a mile of smooth stone straight up."

"I climbed a hedge of thorns partway, then used a rope and grappling hook."

I sawed through the last strands and handed back his knife. "You can go back the way you came, or out the door like a normal person, but I'm going to find out what on earth's the matter with the maids and guards." I yanked the door handle.

It didn't budge.

I pulled again.

"Wood's swollen, probably," Phillip tapped around the doorframe.

"It worked fine yesterday." I'd swooshed out in my shimmery rose ballgown, ready for feasting and dancing.

Then what'd happened?

I shook my head to loosen sleepy thoughts. "Will you help, please?"

Phillip nodded. "On the count of three."

On three, we pulled together, and the door flew open, flinging me against Phillip's chest. Face hot, I pushed off him and hurried out of the room.

Two guards leaned against the wall, yawning. Their long beards flowed over rusty armor. When they saw me, they grabbed at their spears.

"When your shift has ended, prioritize haircuts, polish your armor, and clean yourselves up."

Phillip eyed me.

"And... have Mizzi draw a bath and fetch the royal manicurist." I swept down the corridor, coughing as my robe kicked up dust.

Phillip's booted footsteps echoed behind me, and my unease grew as I passed unlit torches and benches covered with grime. Garlands of birthday ribbons hung from the banisters, their royal purple faded to an insipid lilac.

"Where are we headed?" Phillip touched my arm, seemingly unfazed by the whole silent-as-a-grave castle thing.

"To my parents' chambers, though you might want to make yourself scarce. The dungeons are designed for maximum discomfort and, no offense, you don't look the fighting-off-the-entire-royal-guard type." His clothes were way too shiny.

"I fought a dragon—"

"Save it, you'll need all the help you can get with Dad."

We turned the corner. Relief rushed through me as my parents hurried from their bedchamber, arms outstretched. "Rory, you're all right!"

I buried my face in Dad's chest, feeling like myself for the first time since waking. "Everything's so strange—"

"Your royal highnesses, thank goodness! Everything's worked out just as we hoped." Flora, my favorite fairy godmother, flitted down the hallway. "The prince has rescued the kingdom after a hundred years."

"We certainly owe you, young man." Dad stretched his hand toward Phillip.

"Hold on, Dad." I stepped between them. "He was in my bed— Wait a minute. Did you say *a hundred years*?"

Flora laughed nervously. "We were just trying to counteract the curse, dear. When you pricked your finger, you were supposed to die, but we put you to sleep instead, until—"

"I've been asleep for *a hundred years*?"

"And the whole kingdom with you."

I sucked in air. Phillip slid a bench over, and I sank into it. "I'm 116."

"Only sort of," Phillip shrugged.

"What about Chiswell?"

"I was trying to tell you. Chiswell's my great-great grandfather."

Dead. I swallowed. We never even held hands.

"His descendant has done us a great service. Young man, I hope you'll consider my daughter's hand suitable recompense." Dad pumped Phillip's hand.

Flora and Mum applauded.

Phillip grinned, until he looked at me.

I stood. "*Celebrating*, people? I'm 116, my betrothed's dead, and you want me to marry some man we found in my bedroom?"

Round eyes stared back.

"No offense, Phillip." I patted his arm. "I'm sure you're a nice guy when not sneaking into bedrooms, but…"

Awkward silence.

Suddenly it was all way too much, way too soon after waking up. I spun around, shaggy hair swishing.

"I'm going back to bed."

THE LOST CITY OF LYONESSE

Ronnell Kay Gibson

Seven-year-old Oliver didn't know why he and his father had run from town, stolen a sailboat, and were fleeing the coast of Land's End, but he knew it wasn't good. It was never good.

This unending cycle of being chased by and eluding the law hadn't always been their life. If Oliver really concentrated, he could remember his father, Thomas, working in his blacksmith's shop and his mother's tender hugs. But four years ago, a fire took his home, his mother, and his father's livelihood. While rescuing Oliver, Father's hands were burned and deformed. Since then, no one would hire him, forcing him to spend the days begging and stealing. Oliver imagined their sprint today had something to do with that.

Oliver breathed in the salty air of the Celtic Sea with relief... at least for the moment. Rest and safety were short-lived.

Oliver tugged on Father's sleeve. His way of asking questions. Though Oliver never spoke, Father always knew what he was thinking.

Father lifted his face to the sunshine. "We're going to the Isles of Scilly." He grinned at Oliver, showing off crooked teeth. "For a new start."

Father pulled a document from inside his patched jacket. "I got me a wharf job. And there they ain't gonna care about my hands."

He put the paper away, but not before Oliver noticed the name at the top was not Father's. *What had he done to get those papers?*

His blood ran cold. Hope, too, was short-lived.

"And then we're gonna get you the best doctors."

Even if Oliver could, he'd never tell Father it was fear that kept him silent. Fear that if he made a sound, they'd be found out and Father would be taken away, too. Now, he wasn't sure he remembered how to speak.

Seeing Father's eyes bursting with expectation, Oliver wanted to believe this time would be different. He silently prayed this opportunity would work out for Father and for the chance to have a real home. *Maybe God'll hear my prayers this time.*

Suddenly the slapping waves against the boat grew fierce.

Father cried, "Hold on tight, Son."

Oliver tied himself to his seat as whitecaps splashed over the side. The higher they swelled, the more the boat groaned and rocked.

Just as Oliver thought they would surely collapse into the sea, they hit land. Though it seemed more like the land hit *them.*

Father peered over the side, as an island rose up underneath them. "What's this?"

The land stretched as far as Oliver could see in every direction, with no evidence that it had just been submerged underwater. It was a lush green, with pasturelands, trees, sheep... and in the distance was a village.

Oliver tugged on Father's sleeve.

"No, this isn't the Isle of Scilly." He jumped out and reached to help Oliver. "This is something much more magical."

Faint church bells caught Oliver's ear.

With a shout, Father grabbed him and spun him around. "We've done it, Son! We've found the lost city of Lyonesse!"

Oliver had heard stories of the famed city. The legend was the city would rise up from the water when it had a purpose to fulfill. Oliver smiled. *My prayer.*

As they hiked into town, the villagers welcomed them into their community as long-lost friends. Oliver and his dad happily accepted food, clothes, a room at the inn, and a job for Father at the bakery. For the first time, Oliver got the chance to attend school and make friends.

One evening after the first harvest season was over, Oliver heard Father slink out in the middle of the night. He laid awake with tightness in his chest till Father came home just before dawn. Later that morning, when Oliver left for school, puddles coated the ground, like it had rained overnight, yet it hadn't.

The next day, his father hurried into their room and quickly closed the door, his pockets bulging. When they went down for the evening meal, Father couldn't look any of their new friends in the eye.

Oliver's heart shattered.

He's back to thieving.

Father had always said he stole only for them to live. *Lies.* Here in Lyonesse he didn't have to steal, but he did it anyway. *It's who he is.*

The next morning, they woke to the whole town under two feet of water. Though the villagers went about their business as usual, Oliver knew... the island was sinking, and it was all Father's fault.

When his father left for work, Oliver skipped school and went back to their room. Maybe if he could find the stolen items, he could return them and then the island would stop sinking.

But before he could look, the inn shook. Oliver hurried

downstairs, but there was no one there. Outside there was no one anywhere. The ground continued to tremble, as the water started rising.

"Oliver!"

He turned to see Father waving him over. "We have to get to the boat."

Panic engulfed him as they sloshed their way toward the outskirts of town, then had to swim the rest of the way. Just as they were about to reach the boat, the island disappeared, creating a swell that pulled Oliver down with it.

He flailed his arms about, trying to break the hold. His lungs burned as the surface grew farther away. *Please let me go. He needs me.*

The island responded with a burp, and Oliver soared to the surface. Father grabbed him and pulled him into the boat and held him tight.

Oliver pushed Father away. With trembling lips, he spoke for the first time in four years. "Thisss... es... all... yor... fault."

Pride then shame flushed Father's face. "You're right, Son. We had our second chance and I blew it."

Father grabbed and ripped up the document still hidden in his pocket.

"You are my second chance. And from now on I'm not going to waste it."

In the distance, church bells sounded.

REMEMBER ME AS VICTORIOUS

Rebecca Morgan

Joyful laughter fills the air as my men arrange carts filled with their wives, children, and the spoils of war at the edge of the battlefield. Their families need to be here to witness when Briton claws her way from the eagles' talons.

I can almost taste victory on my tongue, sweet and savory as spiced honey, as I smear woad over my face. It buzzes through the air. Through the land under my feet.

"Heanua. Lannosea. My daughters." I kiss their own woad-smeared foreheads. "Remember today as the day we shake off Roman rule."

They nod, eyes proud and hard. True Celtic women.

My men stand side by side, packed together in the narrow field. Voices of danger whisper to me, but I push them out of my mind. Grasping my sword, I lift it above my head. The scars across my back pull taut, a reminder of why I am here.

"Camulodunum, Verulamium, Londinium. They've fallen beneath the Iceni's hands. Barbarians they call us. Inferior. *Non-Roman*. Nothing is safe from their pride and arrogance. No more will they take our lands. Our island. We far outnumber the Roman dogs. Victory will be ours. May the gods remember us this day."

Alpin, my Druid advisor, lifts a cup of sheep's blood in the air.

"May the gods remember us." He pours it over himself. On the ground. Our land drinks the sacrifice.

He looks at me and smiles. "The gods have heard and seen. You are blessed, Boudicca."

Lifting my sword higher, I let out a battle cry. My men join me one by one till the land shakes beneath our feet. I turn to face the Romans. To lead us to victory.

The Romans advance first with their neat rows, shields held high. I signal my archers to release their poisoned darts. The sky darkens as the arrows sail through the air, carried by the breath of the gods.

As one, the Romans raise their shields, covering their heads. As expected, many of the arrows bounce harmlessly to the side. Bloodcurdling screams tell me some have found their mark.

The red mass advances. No matter. Battles aren't won in the beginning.

My own wave moves next. Chests painted. Hair braided in tight ropes. These are the ones most loyal to me. The strongest.

The front line of Romans kneels, protecting their comrades with shields as they let a storm of javelins loose.

"Cover!" I cry, the word passing from mouth to mouth as we kneel, shields above our heads. But an eye for an eye. My men die before me as the javelins find homes among them.

Death long ago stopped bothering me. We have won before. We shall win again.

The Romans advance, pushing us back farther. Bodies press in, squeezing together. Heat radiates off them.

The field is too narrow. There is nowhere to go.

Panic sinks her claws into my bones.

Arrows fly. Javelins fall.

My men cry out, their cries fracturing my heart.

Death surrounds me.

I can no longer see my daughters.

My ears roar as the world rushes by. Alpin deflects a deadly blow from skewering me.

Fight. For Pritani.

The gods have blessed me. They will not fail.

Hand wet with blood, my sword slips from my grasp. I lose it among the fray. A dagger it is.

My men struggle for room to wield their swords. They trip, fall, and are crushed beneath the masses. The bodies begin to pile.

This is a horrendous defeat.

Defeated. Run.

"Retreat!" I scream. But we cannot.

We can't move. The mass of men pushes. Shoves. Scratches, bites, and claws. But there is no place to go. Our way is stopped by the carts filled with loot, women, and children.

We shall die by our own arrogance. The gods have abandoned us.

Screams rend the air with death. Screams of wives with no husband to protect them. Children calling for fathers.

Seventy-thousand and more have died by my hand. I spared none. And the Romans will repay. The feral instinct to live runs rampant. "Heanua! Lannosea!" My daughters hear my call and weave among the slain, straining to reach me. And I abandon my men who call for me. Whose dying hands reach out to grasp my clothes.

"My queen." Alpin kneels before me. My daughters stand at my side, tears falling silently.

"Don't," I whisper. The Iceni have fallen. I know it in my bones. Because my heart and blood and sinew are tied to my island. A union of souls.

But I have failed her. Divorced her. Left her when she most

needed me.

Abandoned my men. As I, their queen, ran and left them behind. I who took them there. The thought is more bitter than the hemlock that will soon coat my tongue.

Alpin smiles sadly, handing me a cup. "I regret nothing, Boudicca. I would have followed you to the end."

"You already are." I laugh bitterly.

He hands my daughters cups as well, taking the last for himself.

This is a noble way to die, truly. Saving myself and my daughters from whatever the Romans have in store. But it's not how I would have chosen. Cowering from my enemies instead of gloriously in battle.

"The Romans are close."

There is no hiding from the Empire. Their arm is long and fingers grasping.

The four of us raise our glasses in a toast of farewell.

This isn't a defeat. This is victory. Dying how I choose.

Victory isn't emerging with power and might. Victory is the small things. Speaking when fear wants you to be silent. Defending what or who you love. Rising from ashes. Making life anew.

May the world remember me as victorious over shame and humiliation.

May the Iceni and Pritani rise again from Rome's oppression.

We drink.

They have found us, bursting through our shelter. Shouting. Cursing. Hands reaching.

But I'm beyond their reach. Now and forever.

Remember me.

LEGENDARY

THE SEA'S MERCY

Maia Rebekah

"Are you the Beowulf who took on Breca in a swimming match on the open sea?"

The festive hall quieted. Unferth, that envious rat, who had remained silent throughout the hero's introduction, now sought to sow discord. Beowulf's boasts had convinced King Hrothgar, and everyone else in the mead hall, that he'd be the one to slay the mighty Grendel.

Everyone except Unferth, apparently.

"You vied for seven nights," Unferth continued, "and then he outswam you, came ashore the stronger contender."

Beowulf grinned. Already, the louse spoke wrong.

"So Breca made good his boast upon you and was proved right. No matter, therefore, how you may have fared in every bout and battle until now, this time you'll be worsted. No one has ever outlasted an entire night against Grendel."

Silence filled the hall.

My turn, thought Beowulf.

"Well, friend Unferth, you have had your say. Although it was mostly the beer that was doing the talking." The court laughed, and he let the sound fade before continuing. "The truth is this: I was the strongest swimmer of all."

Well, second strongest.

Another icy wave tumbled over Beowulf. The saltwater stung his eyes and skin and clung to his beard in frosty beads. Only one night had passed since he and Breca had begun their race, and already his armor pulled at his bones, dragging him beneath the surface. If only he could slip out of the chainmail, then he'd leave his friend leagues behind. Before he could even consider stopping, though, something yanked him into the depths.

His numbed fingers fumbled to draw his sword. The darkness of the water was nearly complete, so he slashed at the tentacled shadow gripping his ankle. The severed arm writhed and released him, its blood darkening the water even more. Three more took its place.

Barbs dug into his calf, and he nearly screamed. Dazed and crushed by both depth and demon, Beowulf stabbed wildly. His last blow found flesh, and the sea-brute slid away. Only by his gracious Lord's design did he have the strength to claw back to the surface. Blessed air filled his lungs as he glanced around. Breca was now only a speck against the boiling waves.

Gasping in the sea-spray, Beowulf swam on.

When darkness fell again, and the sea quieted, Beowulf nearly caught up with Breca.

Although the moon was waning, brilliant blue and green motes swirled around him, lighting his way and giving him strength. Massive, monstrous shadows lurked far beneath the luminescent water, but they seemed loath to leave the darkness. Beowulf determined to use their inattention to his advantage and make up for lost time.

"*Greetings, glittering man of the shore.*" A woman's voice, clear and bright as the water, trilled inside his skull.

Unable to speak without taking in mouthfuls of sea, Beowulf answered in his mind, just as he'd heard. *Greetings. Might you show yourself, maiden?*

A flash of golden scales broke the water before him. A woman, with ice-white arms and a fish-tail armored in the most precious gold, gazed at him with black eyes. *"I have followed you this night and day. You swim slowly and far from land. How have you come all this way, wearing heavy scales?"*

Beowulf halted and treaded water, drinking in this creature's beauty. Her hair was long and black, unlike the pale yellow of the womenfolk of his homeland.

I am Beowulf, son of Ecgtheow. I have had many great triumphs. Now, I wish to conquer the sea and best my friend in a test of stamina and strength. My hard-ringed chainmail protects me from the teeth of those sea-brutes who would feast on my flesh and hinder me on my journey.

"I see. I am Leohta, Njord's kin."

Would you seek to hinder me as well, Sea-Daughter? I confess I shall have a harder time slaying such a beautiful maiden than all the treacherous whale-beasts in these waters.

"Nay, I shall not hinder you. Your scales caught my eye; I mistook you for one of my kinsmen, strayed from home." She blinked her white-less eyes. "Might I bless you, instead?"

I would have an addled brain to decline your blessing, sweet creature.

She plucked a scarlet sphere from a pouch belted to her waist and pressed it to his lips. *"Consume this."*

He bit down. The strange fruit burst, sending bitter liquid running down his throat. He fought not to gag. The potion warmed his innards, and his lungs began to burn.

Have you poisoned me?

"No. I have blessed you." Her cold fingers stroked his cheek. *"May you reach land alive and whole."* With a splash, she left Beowulf alone in the glowing sea.

The next night, he faced several more frightening creatures of the dark deep, but he could hold his breath longer and easier. He even strove beneath the water for hours without the need of air. This new ability—this blessing—was his salvation. Countless beasts eagerly pulled him far into their dens, smothering him, pinning him with spines and teeth. But each one, he bested with the aid of Leohta's gift.

Beowulf ended his tale to Hrothgar, keeping Leohta's divine blessing and gift to himself, his secret joy.

"Worn out as I was, I survived those five nights, came through with my life. Breca may have won the race, but he encountered only one beast. My sword hurled nine back into the abyss. Now, I cannot recall any fight you entered, Unferth, that bears comparison. In fact, if you were truly as courageous as you claim to be, Grendel would never have gotten away with his unchecked slaughter."

Face ablaze with obvious shame, Unferth stood and left the hall, much to the amusement of Hrothgar and his court.

The coward's challenge had only served to heighten Beowulf's grandeur in Heorot, yet to Beowulf, it served as a reminder of a debt of gratitude he could never repay.

A MISTAKE BY ANY OTHER NAME

Elizabeth Arceo

"One hundred fifty-four. To name something is to decide its fate.

"The Holy Nym named this world, its peoples, and their future. The titles and epithets given by Him and others have insurmountable power and are inherently perfect—"

Errorin brazenly scribbled the word "perfect" out. *Freeing me from my name would be "perfect."*

But Tutor Allread would never accept scribbled lines; the welts on Errorin's neck taught her that much. She relaxed her hand, restarting her lines on a new parchment.

Her back ached from sitting on the wooden stool since morning. She almost slouched but didn't want to draw the tutor's crow eyes. His hard words bruised as deeply as his stick did. Besides, if he thought her petulant, he might bell her father again.

Lord Allgain's forbidding words from that morning still rung in her ears. *Veritan citizens never undermine their true name.* Her tearful explanations, accompanied by her half-sisters' giggling, stayed unacknowledged as her tutor delivered Father's punishment.

Even now, Errorin's misery amused them, for when Tutor Allread left the study, Goldin and Brighteye leaned closer to her stool.

"It's your own fault, *Errorin*—persuading us to call you Darkhair or Wordless? That's sinful!" Goldin's honeyed voice stung more than the welts.

Brighteye smiled unkindly. "Our lovely mother can barely look at you. Admit it! Errorin's the perfect name for you. The *perfect* name for Mother's mistake."

Her half-brother Pureworth stood abruptly, jostling his desk. "Can you two shut your UnNamed mouths for once!"

Errorin grinned as her half-sisters fled the study, probably to snitch, but no one ever punished Pureworth; everyone loved him—even Errorin.

He brushed off her sniffled "Thanks," and crouched next to her. "Don't listen to them. You are who you are, and that's my sister."

"But they're right... I'm a *bastard*, a mis—"

"They're wrong, sister, and you'll know that someday."

....

Wind sliced through her many layers. Prepared as she'd come after learning about the Appellation Mountains, the books had understated how lethal the temperature would be at this altitude.

She couldn't fathom water boiling in those winds, but her uncertainty motivated her to keep moving. If unseen forces heated the water, perhaps the legends spoke truth about the lake's powers.

The unforged path she'd mapped over years of research finally began to descend into fog. If her navigation held true, she'd find a boiling lake through the mists. Legends say the Nym flooded the glen, destroying the greatest temple to the UnNamer ever built.

Every Nameless follower within drowned, but the resulting lake retained the priests' alleged powers.

The ability to UnName.

Her boot slipped, and the sharp decline dragged her down. Ice, rocks, and roots bruised and tore at her before she finally slammed into a boulder.

Szzzzzzsss.

A wave of heat warmed her dampened clothes as she found her knees in a haze of pain. The fog dissipated near the jagged edge's tumultuous water, and her breaths, already short from the altitude, abandoned her. Her head grew lighter each moment she wondered at the mythic waters of Appellation Lake.

Years seeking the lake had earned her scholarly accolades, entrance to the prestigious Vanitas University, but also endless hardship. All the gritted teeth under jeers, all the fisted hands under robes, and all the pinned-on smiles… Finally, they'd led to her freedom!

Her pitiful, disdainful name could finally be burned away in this watery fire. The steam filled her lungs as her breath returned— as did her purpose.

Using a flint, her torch *fwooshed* to life after much battling with the elements. She rose to survey the water's edge until she found a place to leverage her weight—close enough to submerge her arm but keep the rest of her body unharmed.

The livid waters seemed to growl and spit at her as she hurried along its banks.

Eventually, she found a suitable ledge and began rolling her right arm's sleeve, baring the scrawling inkstain "ERRORIN" to the bitter wind.

Propping the flame against the boulder, she bit down on her right glove, tugging leather off numb fingers. Her bare hand drifted closer to the agitated surface that seemed to absorb the flickering light.

The living water leapt to meet her, welcoming her flesh like any Nameless to their Order. The invitation's scalding teeth bit into her palm, and she recoiled.

Icy dread cooled her intentions like the wind at her back. Could she reach her whole arm into the liquid fire? According to the stories, the ritual to UnName included staining the name into your skin and, despite a stain's permanence, burning the inkstain off in the boiling lake.

Her chapped lips recited archaic words. "As burned flesh heals to reveal unblemished skin, the world will heal to reveal unblemished memory."

They must forget Errorin—then, she can be free.

Clenching her naked arm, she recited the ritual she'd memorized long ago. Her quickened breaths began racing.

"I am Errorin of House Everhigher, Daughter, Sister, and Friend to many in that house." She kneeled, eyes gazing into the void boiling below her. "I am Student, Scholar, Seeker, Finder." She grasped for the many names that made her who she was, "I am Hurt, Desperate, Angry." She lowered her head. "A Mistake…"

As she glared into the rippling abyss, the torchlight flickered over her face, and she saw herself without the bitter truths. "But also Earnest, Clever, and Generous." In the swirling black, she saw classmates who'd liked her. "Appreciated." She saw a household that respected her. "Honored." A brother who cared for her. "I am Loved." A single tear fell and sizzled.

She saw a future that Errorin had built for herself despite winds of hatred.

Her breath caught.

"I am Mistaken, but I am *not* a Mistake."

She fell back from the unwelcoming water, holding her frozen arm to her chest—the inkstain no longer a blemish.

Bruised and unsteady, Errorin of House Everhigher rose, turned from Appellation Lake, and trudged back to her life—to *Errorin's* life.

X

LEGENDARY THINGS

BIFROST

Laurie Herlich

I watch the sun rise through the mist, creating an early morning rainbow. The colors glow, and in my awe, I forget the mug I hold. The clatter shatters my reverie, and I blink at the shards on the concrete. I will sweep that up later. For now, I am lost in wonder contemplating Bifrost, and the Norse legend of a rainbow bridge. On his eight-legged horse, Odin would travel that bridge between Earth and Asgard, their version of heaven.

Tears sting my eyes. The doctors must have a way to keep Timmy from crossing that bridge. They must. I straighten my shoulders. This is why we moved across the country—to get better medical care for Timmy. I am so grateful for the way God moved to have us inherit this lovely old farmhouse right when we needed it.

I hear a frightened cry. The narrow staircase creaks as I take the stairs two at a time. I lift Timmy from his crib and clasp him in my arms, smoothing his damp hair and cooing to him. He relaxes and looks up at me with tears lingering in his blue eyes.

"Momma, I hear horsies."

I spin slowly around, gazing at the 360-degree mural in what Aunt Marie appropriately calls the Cowboy Room.

"Hush, my sweet. Of course, you were dreaming of horsies.

Look at all the cowboys and horses around you. Here's your cowboy hat and you've already got your Roy Rogers pj's on. I'll cook us a real cowboy breakfast."

Bacon and egg burritos take just a few minutes to cook up. I look up as I bring the fragrant, steaming platter to the table. My small son is astride his rocking horse, the springs give him a ride like a bucking bronco. He waves his cowboy hat in the air and giggles with glee.

Later, Timmy cries and shies away from being poked and prodded by new doctors. I whisper softly, "Just a little more and we can visit some real horsies."

The shadow of a smile curls the edges of his lips.

That afternoon, waving at the horses through the fence wipes his tears away. My tears are not as easily soothed; the doctors are not encouraging with their prognosis.

Shortly after midnight, I hear Timmy calling for me again. I rush into his room. "Hush, my darling, it's just a dream. Momma's here now."

"Momma, I hear horsies laughing, and they come right up to me. Momma, they are so big!"

"You must be remembering the horses we saw this afternoon."

"They're real, Momma. They sniffled at me with their big, big noses. The cowboys asked me if I wanted to ride on the white one."

Timmy snuggles into my shoulder. I find the rocking chair in the dark and soothe him back to sleep. His little body relaxes, and I place him into bed.

I creep back to my own bed, praying for my little son. A cool breeze drifts from the open window; I pull up my blanket and am asleep before I know it.

I awake to the sun and to my bed bouncing like a bucking bronco.

"Timmy, how did you get out of your crib?" *Did I leave the guard down last night?*

"The cowboys let me out, Momma."

"The cowboys?"

"The ones in my room."

My little cowboy has such vivid dreams. At least he is not as preoccupied with his medical issues as I am.

"Come, sweetie. I'll make us breakfast, and we can visit the real horses after the doctor."

"No doctor, Momma. Just horsies."

My cowboy rides the hobby horse, not quite as vigorously as yesterday, but he still manages to wave his cowboy hat in the air.

The doctors are even less encouraging. They recommend we call hospice in the morning. We visit the horses again. Timmy doesn't even climb down from my arms, but he waves to the steeds.

As I put him in bed, something catches my attention. The side of the crib is down, but I didn't lower it. How could Timmy have figured that out? My eyes travel to the cowboy mural. Was there always a rainbow over the dusty trail? Worry is playing mind games with me. I place my weary cowpoke in his bed.

"I love you, Momma. I will tell the cowboys you say howdy to them."

"I love you, Timmy. Have pleasant dreams. I will see you in the morning."

"I'm gonna ride the white horse tonight, Momma."

I kiss his soft cheek.

I can hardly breathe, never mind sleep, hiccupping and gasping for air between sobs.

Before dawn, I climb the stairs to check on Timmy. He lies peaceful and still under his covers when I lean through the doorway, and I release a soft sigh. I wait a moment more, listening for his breathing. But there is none. I can hardly catch my own breath, and I rush to his side.

I check his pulse and clasp him in my arms. His little body is cold and still, and I hold him as tightly as I can. My heart thumps in my chest, and my breath comes in gasps. My tears run down my cheeks and wet my little boy's hair. How can he be gone already?

Did I hear a horse whinny? I hear a giggle and turn around slowly. There, on the mural is a white horse galloping away. On his back rides a tiny cowboy, waving his hat in the air.

I sit heavily in my rocking chair, listening to the rain, holding my sweet son for one last night. As the sun rises, the mist creates another rainbow. Bifrost. I imagine my little cowboy riding his white horse up the bridge to heaven.

RELIC RECOVERY LEAGUE

Rachel Ann Michael Harris

Widow, single mother, and, now, unhireable. Amelia dropped the phone in her purse, pushing away the recent email from the museum turning her down for their current position. Over fifteen years out of the archeology field made her a relic in the industry. And with the insurance running low, she'd have to cut back to the essentials. Which meant Luke's music lessons would have to go.

Amelia watched as her son sat in the sanctuary after his faith formation class had ended, waiting for her grief support group to finish.

Lord, will this ever end?

She couldn't fall apart. Forcing a smile, she marched up to her son and clasped her hands together. "Ready to go?"

"Sure. How was your group?"

She sighed. "Howard had a hard time. Father Mike had to take him aside."

As Luke gathered his books, his faith formation notebook fell to the floor. Amelia picked it up and recognized five bars of roughly-made sheet music filling its pages.

"Learned a lot tonight?"

He pointed at the notebook. "That totally relates to what we were discussing."

"*Mh-hm.*" She passed it back with a sidelong stare. "Why don't—"

The church suddenly shook violently, nearly tossing Amelia and Luke to the ground. It passed as quickly as it came.

"Was that an earthquake?" Luke asked, his voice trembling like an aftershock.

Across the sanctuary, St. Helena's portrait, their church's patroness, hung askew on the wall. Luke ran across the sanctuary to fix it.

"Wow, look at this." Luke pulled on the frame.

Amelia realized that it wasn't crooked but had swung open on hinges. Behind the portrait was an elevator door. Luke hit the down button, and the doors opened with a ding. Chuckling, he stepped inside.

"Luke, get out of *there*." Amelia's voice pitched in panic as she imagined the elevator plummeting out of sight.

"This is so cool," he said instead.

As the doors began to close, Amelia quickly jumped inside. It began a long, steady descent. When it reached the bottom, the elevator dinged and the doors slid open again. Amelia blinked and leaned out. Rows upon rows of shelves stretched out before her in a concrete bunker filled with ancient artifacts. Even at a distance, her experienced eye told her many of them were from the early Christian period or even earlier.

She stepped out of the elevator. "What in the world..."

"How did you two get down here?" Fr. Mike stood near the corner of one of the shelves. "Fr. Patrick is going to be very upset when he finds out," he muttered to himself. "You need to go."

"Is this what caused that shake?" Luke stood by a large, gaping hole in the floor.

Amelia wrapped her arms around her son, moving him away from the edge as she gazed into the bottomless pit.

"Unfortunately," Fr. Mike confirmed. "Hurry. He could come back any minute."

Mind swimming and heart pounding, Amelia pulled Luke away and followed the priest. "Who might be back?"

"Howard. I thought one of our relics could help, but instead he ran off with Moses's Staff."

"Moses's Staff? As in—"

"Exodus. Plagues. Water from rocks. Giant holes in the ground," Luke rattled off.

Before Fr. Mike could respond, they rounded an aisle just as Howard came around another with the elevator between them. The older man clutched a wooden staff in his hands, glancing between them like a frightened animal ready to strike.

Instead, he raised the staff and brought it down on the floor. Water gushed out and flowed across their feet, sweeping their legs out from under them and sending them sliding toward the pit. Flailing at the passing shelves, they snagged the legs of metal shelving units before reaching the pit's edge.

"Howard, please," Fr. Mike pleaded. "Have mercy—"

"Mercy?" Howard screeched. "Did that drunk driver have mercy when he ran over my wife? He received mercy when the review board granted him early release."

Amelia swallowed, imagining her husband's warm arms around her shoulders. And the cold emptiness that hung there now. Stolen from them too soon, too.

"Now he'll experience the wrath of true justice"—he raised the staff—"when he's eaten by the ground upon which he walks."

As he reached for the elevator button, sweet tones of string music filled the bunker. The tune wrapped around Amelia and soaked into her heart, breaking away years of heartache. Tears welled in her eyes as a torrent of emotion poured out. The sorrow swallowed her while the song crescendoed, bolstering hope and giving her strength to go on.

Howard choked, crying in anguish and doubling over as his grief returned. The staff dropped to the ground as he collapsed.

"I'm sorry." Howard wept.

Fr. Mike snatched the artifact.

A hand rested on Amelia's shoulder and she turned to see Luke with a harp in his hand and tears in his eyes.

"David's Harp. I thought, it helped Saul, maybe it could help Howard, too."

The elevator dinged and Fr. Patrick stepped out. After glancing at each of them, he turned to Fr. Mike. "What happened?"

"In sum, we gather, protect, and, when appropriate, use these relics to bring God's mercy where we're led. Having someone who is familiar with not only the biblical but also historical knowledge of the relics would be quite useful."

Amelia glanced at the job application on Fr. Patrick's desk. After what she'd just seen, could she place herself in danger like this?

Are you leading me here, Lord?

Luke picked up the application. "Can I join?"

"Of course," Fr. Patrick said. "God calls across all ages."

Amelia snatched the application from Luke as she gave the priest a sidelong glare.

"But," he went on, "we should never forget the fifth commandment."

Lord, please let this be the right path. Picking up a pen, Amelia finished the application and passed it back.

Fr. Patrick smiled and reached out his hand. "Welcome to the Relic Recovery League."

NO MORE TEARS

Abigail Falanga

Tari watched incense drift to the ceiling. After the ceremonies ended, when the artificial gravity automatically shut down, the fragrance would fill the pyramid—weaponized by the addition of a toxic compound. The haze would obscure the gold and precious jewels that glimmered from every surface, deterring any grave robbers who made it past the complex security system guarding the inner burial room.

Tari brought her mind back to the present. She knew the chants by heart but found her groans and ululations lacked emotional fervor if her mind drifted.

She added an extra sob.

The family grouped around the elaborately inlaid coffin, looking almost as bored as she felt. The deceased, embalmed in the traditional way with organs tucked in canopic jars for the journey through the afterlife, had been a youth who'd wasted his life on luxury and willfulness. Few would miss him.

The chants ceased. Mourners shuffled away. His mother laid a lingering hand on the sarcophagus, eyes red.

Good.

If their efforts had awakened sentimentality in the mother's heart, she'd tip well, perhaps tell others how moving the funeral had been.

It was good for business.

Tari and her colleagues waited a few minutes in respectful silence as the priests performed the last rituals and left. Then Tari pulled a fold of her white gown up to wipe her eyes and rose.

Unfortunately, it was Tari's turn to stay behind and set mourning seals in place while the rest of the party—family, friends, priests, attendants, and professional mourners—shared a funerary feast on the cruiser.

Pity. The feasts were the best perk of this job.

Tari waved her colleagues off from the docking bay as the cruisers drifted into the Nile Ways, which connected the systems of the Interstellar Egyptian Kingdoms. The other two pyramids were visible, gleaming gold in the starlight. They were beautiful, massive monuments to wealth—tombs of the royal families.

But there was work to be done before she took the small company shuttle back to base on Delta 1.

Incense wafted toward her. Tari choked a bit and waved it away.

Tidy up linens, set three seals—

Was that a noise?

Tari peered into the haze of the third chamber. She was supposed to be alone. Even the priests had gone. Still…

"Hello?" she called. "Is someone there?"

No answer.

She shook her head and packed away the irritants she and her colleagues used to produce tears.

Clunk!

Tari spun around in time to see something—someone—turn the corner.

"You can't be here!" she shouted. "Security locks in soon. You'll be killed."

"You'll be killed," a voice repeated. It was no echo.

Tari stuffed away the last of the paraphernalia. "It's your choice."

"Are you..." came the voice again, "...afraid?"

"I don't have time for this. You want to die, fine." Tari ignored the shiver running down her spine and set the next three seals in place. "If you want a lift, I'm leaving."

"Are you?"

Tari looked around. Still no sign of the weirdo. "Are you coming?"

Silence. Then, "Where are the slaves?"

Tari's mouth went dry. "They outlawed the practice of burying slaves with the dead years ago."

"Then who will carry their riches in the afterlife?"

"Drones are considered more humane."

"But drones shed no tears." The voice was so near that she could feel rancid breath crawl on her skin.

Tari hiked up her skirts, ready to run—or fight. "Who *are* you?"

Nothing.

She set off at a brisk walk toward the docking bay, watching the shadows, cursing whoever thought starlight and dim lamps a good idea. No sound of pursuit, but she *felt* it following.

"The slaves wept as they knew their deaths were approaching."

The voice came so suddenly and just behind her that Tari let out a small scream, nearly jumping out of her skin.

"Their tears were delicious. Powerful. Potent."

"What are you?" she nearly shrieked.

"I'm hungry," it laughed.

Tari ran.

The corridors of the great pyramid seemed endless. Doors slid down behind her as she passed, security protocols sealing them.

Finally, Tari reached the docking bay and skidded to a stop

beside the shuttle airlock.

Was she alone? Had she managed to leave it behind?

She glanced around—and shrank back as something only vaguely humanlike, made of shadow, crawled into the docking bay on limbs too long.

The shuttle.

Tari slammed her hand on the hatch, ready to jump inside the instant the doors opened.

"Error," a computer intoned. "Airlock compromised. Cannot open."

"You can't leave," the *thing* said. "I need your tears."

"I can shed tears for you if that's all you want," Tari hissed. "That's my job—tears on command. Just let me go."

"Not only tears. Grief. Fear. Are you afraid?"

"Terrified!" Tari was shaking, but her sobs were dry.

Something like a lifeless hand crept up her arm and compelled her to turn.

It had no face.

"You have no tears left," it said. "Have you no heart?"

Tari gasped as it pressed onto her face, then withdrew. In its place came memory—of the funeral and how her weeping came not out of pity for the family, like she had once felt, but from practiced artifice. She hadn't cared for a long time.

"Warning," said the computer. "Full security measures engaging in fifteen minutes."

"Please!" Tari whispered. "Let me go. The incense will be weaponized—I'll die."

"Like the slaves," mused the *thing*. "They wept when they realized their fate was sealed."

It withdrew, leaving silence.

Tari turned to the control panel, trying everything she knew, hitting the distress signal only to get static, praying to whatever gods might be listening. Nothing.

"Five minutes until full security."

"Please!" Tari sobbed. A single tear slipped down her cheek.

"Ahhh..." came the hungry voice. "There it is."

A HOLE IN VALHALLA

Pamela Love

Surprises are few here in Valhalla, the afterlife Odin has provided for those worthy warriors slain in combat. As a Valkyrie, I know each fighter by name—generally Sven or Bjorn. I know what they want, too—victory or a fresh opponent for battle each day, and more meat or mead during their nightly feasts.

Yesterday, a warrior approached me, dripping on the dining hall's stone floor. Hardly a rare sight here, except before it's always been blood, sweat, or spilled mead that rendered the footing sticky or slippery. This man... was *clean.*

Bards sing of the heroes of Valhalla, of their courage, capability, and cunning. They never sing of their hygiene. I took a deep breath, unable to believe my eyes—or nose. The effect was striking. In Valhalla's dining hall, between the sweat, grime, and blood from the fighting—all wounds disappear at sunset each day, but the gore remains—and with the lack of table manners or even napkins during the feasts, the stink had seeped into the stone walls.

"Hail, Valkyrie Sigrun! What caused yonder flood to fall upon my brow?" Bjorn the Brave the Forty-Fifth pointed to his empty seat at a nearby table, where a flood was indeed pouring down.

Those sitting beside it were likewise getting an impromptu bath, to their noticeable improvement. Less curious than their comrade, they continued to feast.

I turned my gaze toward Valhalla's roof, which was built of golden shields. One of them was missing. Through that hole flowed a river—one of many—from the antlers of a gigantic enchanted stag, which dwelt on a hill above Valhalla with a mead-giving goat. Yes, I know mead is made from honey. Tell the goat that.

I shrugged. "I knowest not, Bjorn."

Odin showed up at dawn the next day, sloshing through the ankle-deep water we Valkyries had been trying to ignore. The warriors mostly didn't care. "I've commanded the stag to turn his head until you find the shield. Normally I'd have my ravens solve this mystery, but they have other business. Sigrun, this is your quest."

"Allfather, it shall be my privilege to serve you." With a salute, I went to work.

Of course I talked to Loki first.

"You dare accuse me, Valkyrie?"

I shrugged. "Who but the god of mischief would take just one shield?"

Loki raised his eyebrows. "Had I done so, it would only have been to cause the entire roof to collapse. Hmm, now there's a thought." With a concerning twinkle in his eyes, he turned away.

Flipping my braid over my shoulder, I sighed. *A problem for another day.*

Next, I investigated my Thor theory. He had his own dining hall in Valhalla, smaller than that of the worthy warriors, and decidedly less odorous. I hammered my fist on its oaken door and entered when he bellowed to do so.

He sat slouched in a chair beside a magnificent wooden wall carving depicting the time he'd swallowed an ox whole. Ah, art.

I posed my question. Thor blinked. "Why would *I* steal a shield? I have no need of one." He picked up his hammer, Mjolnir. "This keeps me safe in battle."

I nodded. "I did not say you took it. But besides thunder, you are god of all storms. Might one of your winds have blown the missing shield away?"

Thor frowned. "Tempests near Valhalla are forbidden by Odin. I respect the Allfather's wishes."

I sighed. It was time to talk to my third suspect, Sven the Savage the Seventeenth. A newcomer to this realm, ambition radiated from him like heat from the sun.

It was quite a change from the coolness of Thor's hall to the sun-drenched battlefield. I wended my way through the countless single combats, my boots squishing over the filthy, trampled turf.

At last I found the Sven that I wanted to question. He'd just forced his fifth straight opponent to surrender. Noticing my stare, he dropped his sword and swung around to face me, arms akimbo. "What would you have of me, Valkyrie Sigrun?"

Subtlety was not the way of my people. I stretched out my hand. "Valhalla's missing a shield. Do you possess it?"

"If I had it, I would not hide it. I now challenge whichever warrior does! I will face him unarmed." He shook his fists and glared, searching for his unknown adversary. "Come forth, O coward! I shall still triumph!"

The look on his face convinced me. Subtlety wasn't his way either. Besides, shortly afterward I checked with my sisters and confirmed he'd been at his seat boasting all of the previous evening. Sven the Savage the Seventeenth was a great one for bombast, and the competition was fierce in Valhalla. Between devouring boar off the bone and pouring mead down their gullets, the worthy slain tell endless sagas of their valor.

I bit my lip. *I wonder.*

Valhalla lacked a true armory. Weapons and shields lay where they were dropped in untidy piles surrounding the battlefield. The largest was close to the dining hall. Beginning my search there, it wasn't long before I found what I sought—the missing shield, slid into a stack of others of lesser metal, yet equal mettle.

Odin returned that evening. I beckoned to him. "Behold the truant. As part of the hall, it has absorbed myriad tales of courage. No longer will it rest content to be a shingle, however glorious the roof."

Odin smiled. "Arise, valiant defender!" The shield levitated, quivering in readiness. "Henceforth shall you indeed be borne by a warrior in combat. And on the day of Ragnarok, you will be carried by the hero battling at my side."

All very noble. Trouble is, ever since then we've started having problems with other objects in the dining hall. Even the tankards are demanding to join the fray, Odin help us...

AQUA VITAE

Gretchen E. K. Engel

Gift, Montana, Fall 1990

Dark shades block out the light so I can sleep late, because in my dreams I am whole. Every night I hear a voice saying, "Preston, you will walk again."

But this time the voice is vivid, real, and familiar. Uncle Jordan, still dressed in scrubs from the night shift, flips on the ceiling light.

The clock's black-and-white numbers flick over to read 8:34 a.m.

"Huh?" My sleep-crusted eyes squint against brightness. Not a cool way to wake up.

"Isn't that what the person in your dream tells you?" Uncle Jordan stands at the end of my bed.

"Yes. But it's impossible. You know what Dr. Clearsey told me."

Uncle Jordan swaps my wheelchair for my desk chair then sits next to my bed. "My cousin is an excellent neurologist, but the solution isn't medical."

Relying on my arms and abdominal muscles, I maneuver to a seated position. "How exactly is a damaged spinal cord not a medical problem?"

Uncle Jordan places his hand on my leg. Probably a reassuring gesture. Sometimes he forgets I don't have much feeling below my waist. "You know about the pool at Bethesda."

"Are you going to fill your bathtub, carry me upstairs, and swirl the water? God isn't interested in a twentieth-century paraplegic." *Paraplegic.* I hate that word. "The Almighty and I are not on speaking terms."

Uncle Jordan hands me a blue glass vial. The label has "Aqua Vitae" printed on it.

"How did you get this?"

"From the OOM clinic, but you have to be chosen to receive it." Uncle Jordan raises a brow. "Go on, drink it."

"You're sure about this?" Our enemies would stoop to killing if they thought it would stop us. "What if you've been tricked into giving me poison?"

"Hippocratic Oath. Do no harm."

I work the cap loose. Liquid sloshes inside and I sniff it. No odor. A good sign. *Aqua nocens*, the corrupt counterpart to aqua vitae, smells of almonds and ammonia. I've never tasted it, but aqua nocens is supposed to be as bitter as it is addictive. I take a sip then finish the vial. Water purer and sweeter than a mountain stream quenches my thirst.

Uncle Jordan leans against my desk. "You won't get sick and will heal rapidly."

In a heartbeat, sensation returns to my hips, thighs, all the way to my toes. My right shin hurts where I banged it against a table leg the other day. Never thought I'd be glad to feel pain. The egg-sized bruise turns from black and blue, to yellow, to flesh colored. It disappears along with the throbbing.

With one hand braced on the bed and the other on my desk chair, I stand, though that seems like too strong of a word. Flesh hangs over atrophied muscles; I no longer have the legs of a distance runner. My first steps are uncoordinated but become easier.

Uncle Jordan smiles under his Magnum P.I. mustache, except he drives a Porsche not a Ferrari. "I know what you want to do."

I hold out my hand for his car keys.

"Not the 944."

I snap my fingers. "I had to try."

Uncle Jordan pulls a shoebox from the closet. He knows what I've truly longed to do. "I'll be here when you return."

Snagging my cross-country sweats from freshman year and a pair of socks from my dresser, I pull my running shoes from the dusty box. My sweatpants stop just above my ankles on my lanky frame. Maybe I've passed the six-foot mark. As if I care. I'm standing. I can walk again. Drive a stick shift. Be normal. Stepping outside, running becomes a compulsion.

The sun glistens over the Bitterroot Mountains, partly obscured by the cloudy sky. Pine-scented air fills my lungs. My first few steps are slow, but I quicken my pace to a full-out run.

Worship. To most people, it means singing. I'd rather run, thankfulness pouring from me with each breath. Like peeling skin from a sunburn, my anger, frustration, and resentment pull away in dry, flaky strips revealing fresh clean pieces of my soul.

Everyday things are new again. Leaning over the sink to brush my teeth, standing to relieve myself. Fresh from my post-run shower, I button a plaid flannel over my T-shirt. Once again, my blue eyes will be the first thing people notice.

A knock on the door. "May I come in?"

"Sure."

Uncle Jordan sets a hinged white cube the size of a jewelry

box on my desk. "We need to key the lock to your print. Press your index finger to the sensor."

I press the middle of the black square located where the keyhole would be. Crosshatches of red light glow under my finger like a grocery store scanner.

"Guard these. Desperate aqua nocens addicts will stop at nothing to get aqua vitae. It only works on those chosen to take it, but they don't know that."

The box is divided into sixteen spaces and fifteen are filled with blue vials.

"That's a two-week supply with a couple of spares. You drink one vial each morning." He nudges my shoulder. "You need to pack."

"Yeah." I should be happier about seeing my parents. They've been abroad since my accident.

He pulls a suitcase from under the bed. "Let's hurry. I need to finish the ramp."

"Why?"

The ramp was the last thing my parents' house needed for it to be accessible.

"In case your aqua vitae is stolen. Without it your paralysis will return." He pauses. "Also, when all the sources of aqua nocens have been destroyed, the final mission will be to destroy the source of aqua vitae."

"Dad estimates we'll be done within five years." I rub my thighs. "This is temporary?"

"I don't know." Uncle Jordan pulls out his car keys and places them in my hand. "Make the most of the time you have."

FIRE BEAR

Lincoln Reed

After they stole my boots, they tied a necklace of dynamite around my throat.

Georgie, an unkempt prospector who stank like a skunk in a manure pile, knelt into the stream and lifted my pan, surveying its sandy contents as dawn glimmered orange in the fuming mist of Yellowstone hot springs.

"Well, lookah here, Tex." Georgie picked out a golden nugget the size of a huckleberry. "Like that crazy professor figured. The mother lode. I reckon her veins are underneath this volcanic earth."

"Was here first," I pleaded, voice cracking, knees quivering. "You got no right—"

"Claim jumper's what you is," Tex said, floppy hat pulled over his scarred face, an eyepatch hugging his left eye. He poked a Colt 1851 Navy revolver into my ribs. "Bound them hands, Georgie. That's it. Behind his back."

The rope cinched my wrists and cut against my skin. I stood on the rocky earth in tattered socks next to a humble stream leading into a simmering hot spring.

Thieves! My pulse raced in righteous fury. *Animals.*

Steam rose from the soil as if the earth itself was boiling with rage. Evergreen hills observed in silent judgment as Tex aimed his Colt at my donkey, Cletus, my lone compatriot in the vast wilderness, my sole confidant, my only friend.

Fury bubbled within my gut. Mounting fear swelled like a torrential wave cresting, ready to crash. "God as my witness I'll—"

A gun blast reverberated. Cletus toppled with a pained heehaw.

Tex spat tobacco with a spiteful sneer. "Too old to haul a blade of grass, that one."

Time slowed, my vision blurring, tears welling in my eyes as the stoic landscape swallowed the decaying gunshot's song.

Cletus! My dry tongue weighed heavy. My fists clenched. *You'll be avenged.*

The hot spring hissed.

I'll not rest...

A creeping sensation scuttled across my skin. Hairs raised. Sweat dribbled down my forehead. I glared at the prospectors. *I'll haunt you. All your days.*

Blood thickened through my veins as anger clogged my laboring heart. My breath caught in my chest, lungs constricting in a pained wail of anguish.

Hellfire on you demons!

Tex unwound a long strand of fuse and backed away. After he and Georgie reached a safe distance, he motioned me toward the hot spring with his gun. "You'll get your gold, Pilgrim. I hear heaven's got entire *streets* of gold."

A wind gust whistled in my ears, whispering as it swept through the valley, harmonizing with the incessant babbling of the creek. The entire vista seemed abuzz with anticipation. Trees stood like audience members basking in the macabre show.

Tex clicked the hammer back on his revolver and pulled the trigger. A ball of lead screamed, skimming the earth next to my big toe. I instinctively kicked my knees up. Sticks of dynamite bobbed against my chest.

The thieves laughed. "Jump, claim jumper! Dance!"

The hot spring hissed as if alive, teeming with apprehension.

"Get on, now." Tex waved me forward. "Get go'n!"

My heartbeat echoed in my head like a drum announcing a death march.

I teetered on a stone, stumbling into the warm stream, water up to my ankles. My mind ached, ideas churning, plotting methods of escape. No matter how hard I clawed at the rope, I couldn't untie my wrists. And if I ran, I wouldn't evade Tex's surefire aim.

I advanced with deliberate steps toward the spring, where a pool of steaming water glistened as blue as sapphire. Rocks cut against my feet as I swayed, trying to avoid falling or bumping the dynamite.

This... This is the end.

Fate settled on my shoulders, heavy with eternity's impending verdict.

Give me justice. I glanced toward the ancient hills. *Vengeance.*

The scenic caldera responded with a gurgle from the hot spring. A sulfuric aroma filled the air like a stringent perfume. Steam clouded my vision as the broiling water burned through my feet, peeling away the skin with a heat so vicious, pain tore through my limbs like wildfire.

Tex flicked a match to a cigarette, took a long drag.

He lit the fuse.

Seconds later, water sprayed into the air, followed by red flames and molten rock. Fire engulfed me, twisting my bones, consuming me from a doorway beneath Yellowstone, morphing and snapping my frame with the binding poultice of ash and brimstone. A coat of fur decorated the lapping inferno coursing through my chest. Smoke wafted from my nostrils as fangs jutted through my extended jaw. Fingers sharpened into claws with nails like obsidian knives.

My guttural, menacing growl rumbled like boulders thundering down a mountain slope. When I emerged through the smoke, the cigarette tumbled from Tex's slack jaw. A trickle of liquid stained Georgie's pants.

I reared on hind legs as Tex gathered his wits, aimed his gun, and yanked the trigger. My fur absorbed each bullet, dissipating the projectiles like wisps of smoke.

Flames shot from my throat with a deafening roar. A geyser of fire poured from my mouth, engulfing Georgie, licking away his flesh.

Tex cursed. Reloaded his gun.

I sauntered on two paws, standing at full height, waving razor claws, spitting fire through bared teeth. The thieving prospector glared at me with trembling lips.

I devoured him whole, reducing the murderer to a pile of ash.

Afterward, I raced through the timber, leaving a trail of scorched bark and charred earth in my wake until the scent of Georgie returned. Rotten, corroded—another group of prospectors, miles away.

As the sun set, I plodded in their direction, hunting their putrid stench, my rage growing with each stride.

You vandals. Thieves.

I found their site hidden in an outcropping, campfires aglow.

All of them were gold miners. Prospectors. Vagrants.

Killers.

Like a bear from the pit of hell, I charged through the trees, disintegrating the fiends into chaff, an oath in my infernal snarl.

I will roam these lands.

Always searching, your scent in nose.

My jaws hungry for your sins.

SEAFLASH

R. L. Nguyen

Most who sail the sea are afraid of enduring a storm. I'd not be anywhere else for all the gold on all the islands, because I only see him when lightning strikes the ocean.

Raindrops plummet down my neck, each dying quick deaths in the jade-dark waves. Night thickens around me and my coracle bobs beneath, rolling me away from my own ship at my back. My eyes scan the torrent-scarred horizon for the first white flash.

I can never decide whether the lightning draws the ghost vessel from below the surface, or places it there from above. I had asked him once; he said he could not tell. Even when his ten years are up and he can set foot on land again, it's likely the mysteries of my husband's servitude will only come to me like echoes in a seashell. A captured reflection of the ocean and not the ocean itself. But that does not matter when the storm rives the sky and his ship appears.

I press forward—my love is waiting. These oars are not made of a size for a woman, but those who scoff at my strength would cease laughing if they saw me row. Cold rain stings my arms, but they burn with exertion and with hope. Hope keeps us both afloat, him and me. Me, sane when I should be mad; him, alive among the dead.

Another diamond flash illuminates the prow of the ghost ship. How do I look from his vantage-point? Like the souls he ferries to the other side, just before they drown?

Rising over my little boat, fingers of frigid water claw my body and snap, drenching me further. I shake them off, blinking away their icy touch.

You will not have me. I board his ship alive.

The storm laughs back in a crash of thunder, as if it heard me. I hope it can. I hope it tells the sea that it can curse my husband, but not take him from me. For seven years I've cheated it in exchange for the fleeting, forbidden moments we share on board the ship of the lost before he must send me away. I can survive three more.

The next bolt is meant to frighten me, I know it. I spit salt, whipping my soaking locks out of my face and heaving my shoulders back. The sea answers, rearing its head, and for a moment I see the horses the ancients believed pulled Poseidon's chariot.

Do your worst! I'm a fool to shout it, except I've survived its worst already.

Faster than sight, the lightning beacons the way once, twice, a dozen times, helping me even as it threatens me. Thunder crackles, but the roar in my ears warns me of another wave.

Nearly there. With a haul of my arms the boat clambers up a tilted wall of water, tipping upwards as the billow stretches out translucent green. My heart spills out of place and the oars bite into my hands—but with a splash we drop on the other side. A few more strokes...

Wind tackles me. A second swell catches the coracle, and it roils. A third hurls me into midair. The oars tear my skin as the sea sucks them below.

I hit the water.

My body spins downward. Every nerve screams against my gritted teeth. My hand breaks through to the rain-specked air before the sea claims me again, trying to bury me without earth.

No!

The lightning shows me the way up. I climb towards it, hand over hand, kicking myself free, lungs writhing.

Air, air, air...

Air. My head shatters the surface. I gulp oxygen and rain, both burning my throat. Waves pound my body but I am free. Before I find my bearing my shoulder slams against crusted wood. The ship.

Something slaps the water, snaking dark and twisted through the froth. A rope! It slips through my numb fingers, and I snatch again, the effort searing my arm. The coarse hemp scrapes my palm and I cling with all my strength.

The rope tautens, drawing me upwards against the stinging torrent. White light plays like hearth fire on a face above me. I gasp as hands grasp me and I tumble over the side.

His arms tighten around me. Strong. Safe. Warm. Murmuring my name, his hoarse whisper cuts through the bellowing of the gale. His tattered coat circles my shoulders with his familiar smell of salt and smoke.

He leans his head back to gaze at me.

"You shouldn't have come." The trails of wetness on his face are more than the storm's blood, as are those on mine.

"Where else would I be?" I bury my head on his shoulder, and his roughened fingers tangle in my hair.

"Look!"

Calling me out of my shelter, he points out across the distance that nearly swallowed me. The last broken shards of my coracle collapse beneath the ocean's buffeting and disappear.

"Your boat's lost," he says. "Lost at sea." He speaks the words all sailors dread with a fierce quietness.

"What does that mean?" My cheek leaves the sodden linen of his shirt.

"It means you are, too." His fingertips trace the curve of my chin. "On this ship, only those lost at sea can stay aboard."

"What?" I glance from him to the place where the coracle sank, and back again. "I—"

"—can stay." His brow touches mine. I catch my breath.

"Forever?"

"I'm not captain forever." The joy in his voice reaches my bones. I wrap my arms around him, his solid frame the antithesis of the shifting and treacherous ocean. Three years at sea is a short enough voyage, compared with the eternity I've just crossed.

The lightning shines brighter on us than starlight.

LEGENDARY EVENTS

LEGENDARY

THE COLLECTOR

Michael Teasdale

Nobody knew precisely where the relics came from nor how those with the money and power to assemble such collections managed to locate them in the first place.

Yet Hal was certain of one thing—at some point he had robbed and swindled them all.

"Let me guess. You see yourself as a modern-day Robin Hood?" the gray-haired man spat as Hal tightened the ropes around his wrists.

"Not really," Hal mused. "Robin Hood, as I recall, robbed from the rich and gave to the poor." He winked as he slipped the gag over his target's mouth. "Whereas I rob from the rich and sell to the even richer. That's capitalism, right? Who knows? On another day, you might have been my client."

Ignoring the muffled protest of the aging millionaire, Hal wandered to an ornate bookcase and ran his finger along its dusty tomes, eventually finding one that stood out through more prominent use.

"*Prometheus Bound*," he read, tilting the book's spine. A section of the wall slid away, revealing a descending stairwell. Peering into the darkness, Hal flicked on his infrared goggles and glanced back at the fuming millionaire struggling against the ropes. "An ironic choice," he chuckled.

As Hal felt his way down the winding staircase, he tried to remember when he'd first crossed the line from simple underground art thief to hunter of the legendary objects that he hoped would buy him his retirement.

The black market for stolen antiquities was a complicated affair. Every aging collector worth their salt had some nefariously obtained Picasso sketch or illegal Etruscan urn buried away in a vault. It was a smaller, more elite circle that dealt in the true treasures of protohistory. The objects that most dismissed, through arrogance or ignorance, as mere legend.

Was it the Green Armor of Arthurian legend that first made him a believer? Probably not. It was hard to judge the armor's effectiveness at preventing external injury when the client had succumbed to old age a few months after receiving it.

Perhaps it was the sword of Thuận Thiên that he'd stolen for a high-ranking member of the Vietnamese military. Or the Rod of Asclepius taken at the behest of a famous American doctor.

In truth, once the deal was done and the payment rested in his account, Hal had little interest in how the new owners chose to use their ill-gotten treasure.

He reached the bottom of the staircase, scanning the room ahead.

Nothing? No infrared beams? No security cameras?

Of course, Hal reasoned, the upper-mansion with its valuable artwork, pottery, and sculpture was designed to distract from the real prize. The amateur thief might make off with a Caravaggio or Constantin but would never dream of what lay beneath. Still, Hal felt a tiny flicker of unease kindling in the pit of his stomach as he looked upon the sculptures that lined the walls of this hidden basement.

Ugly looking things; certainly, no Renaissance masterworks.

Instead, they appeared to be statues set in peculiar poses, chiseled from rough, unfinished stone. With the night-vision it was hard to get a better look, but his concerns were extinguished when he spied the pedestal at the back of the room and saw the box resting atop it. A crooked smile creased his lips, remembering the words of his contact in Marrakech.

Nobody knows for sure what's inside it, but they say it's power beyond measure. If your client likes the Ancient Greek stuff... well, let's just say you'll never have to work again!

Hal's hands trembled with anticipation as he took hold of the box's lid and carefully raised it. Too late he saw a flash of movement and felt the sharp pain in his wrist.

"Little snake, little snake, oh how you slither." The voice rolled in from some unseen speaker as the lights powered on in a flash of white. Blinded by the sudden glare, Hal wrenched off the goggles and dropped them to the floor as pain raced up his arm.

"Did you really think I wouldn't guard my greatest treasure?"

He recognised the voice now. It was the old man, no longer incapacitated. Hal's vision swam back into focus as his eyes adjusted to the light. He stared into the box.

A head lay in the box, mouth open in a permanent death snarl, a nest of green vipers squirming where the hair should have been. They writhed and hissed and snapped at him. Yet it was the eyes, the terrible burning hatred of the gorgon's eyes, that burrowed into him as the lecture from above continued.

"Isn't she beautiful? The legendary Medusa, slain by Perseus! Full petrification will of course take a moment. She is rather old after all," the voice explained. "Still, it will be long enough for you to admire my *true* collection."

Hal's chest began to stiffen. He could already feel the leaden weight in his legs. He stumbled as the flame of doubt rekindled into an inferno of panic. His eyes darted around the room. *Stupid!* He saw the statues for what they truly were now. The faces frozen in terror. A sea of thieves cast in stone.

"If it's any consolation," the man said, "you will be the pride of my collection, Hal. I've tracked your progress for some time. Your work is most impressive."

"H-How?" Hal stuttered in defeat, vocal cords tightening as the immobilizing petrification crept up past his shoulders.

"Your clients turned you in," he chuckled. "It was simple to lure you here as we did with the others. You've stolen from so many of us that you've become a liability to your own employers. This is the endgame for thieves like you, but don't worry. I've a place along the wall picked out for you."

Hal felt a solitary tear form in the corner of his eye. Before it could roll down his cheek, it was no more than a blemish on The Collector's newest acquisition.

LEGENDARY

LAID BARE

Teddi Deppner

Naked, but for the cloth wrapped around my hips, I began each day in Pithom begging for food outside a stone temple. I had time-traveled to the ancient Earth city to study their mud brick construction techniques. It was truly impressive—and humbling—what a civilization could accomplish in bare feet.

I didn't speak the language, so my efforts relied heavily on playing mute and finding a suitable benefactor. After being chased off the construction site twice, one of the kinder supervisors—a man called Uri—had pity on me and allowed me to help him with simple tasks.

Today, when Uri's broad chest and dark curly hair appeared in the crowd passing the temple, I ran to join him. He handed me a piece of bread and a few dates, which I gratefully accepted. The morning temple-goers had not been generous.

For the rest of the day, I toiled in the early spring sun. I watched the other men and copied them, collecting dry stalks of vegetation from the fields and dumping them into a cart before trotting to find more materials for the brick recipe.

After work I slept under a willow tree by a canal. It was usually an idyllic spot to spend the evening, but a week ago the waterways around town had turned a ruddy hue—some runaway algae bloom, I assumed—and dead fish now floated along the water's edge. The evening breeze dispersed the noxious smell, but the following day a cascade of natural calamities began.

Noisome waters drove hordes of frogs into town.

Then the frogs all died. Poisoned by the red waters, perhaps?

Swarms of biting gnats followed, then clouds of bigger flies. No doubt spawning in the frog carcasses.

I was walking beside Uri's sledge after the insect swarms finally abated when an ox pulling a cart next to us lowed and fell over. Canopic jars from the cart hit the dirt and shattered, spilling pungent oil and human innards across my naked feet.

And I'd thought stepping on frogs was revolting.

Scores of livestock dropped dead all around us that day, probably infected by the flies.

I seriously considered teleporting to a less catastrophic year in Pithom, but curiosity compelled me to stay. This civilization's canals, architecture, and medical acumen were impressive for its time, and I wanted to see how it recovered from the chaos.

My curiosity nearly killed me. I was gathering straw at midday when lightning split the sky and unleashed massive hailstones—crushing crops, man, and beast alike. I took shelter under a tree only to be knocked off my feet by a falling branch.

Then Uri arrived and pulled me up.

We ran like madmen through the deafening storm, seeking shelter from the deadly barrage. I followed him blindly until suddenly the hail ceased. I stumbled to a halt and peered around at undisturbed fields under bright blue sky, my bare skin bloody and bruised.

Just a dozen meters behind us in the twilight under black clouds, a chunk of ice the size of a man's head shattered against a dirt road. Sparkling shards spun out to melt on the sunlit side of the eerie demarcation.

A frisson of terror struck me as I heard my mother's voice in my head.

"—but in the land of Goshen where the Israelites dwelled, not a single hailstone fell."

This singular constellation of events had a name.

The ten plagues of Egypt.

Stunned by this revelation, I let Uri lead me to a mud brick bungalow about a kilometer from the storm. He lodged me in a storage hut perched on the rooftop, and his wife tended my wounds. The days following were a blur.

This couldn't *actually* be happening.

I sat on Uri's rooftop as he left for work, my thoughts whirling. When he returned, his ox dragged a heavily-laden sledge. After an animated conversation, Uri's wife packed the pile of silver and gold platters, stunning jewelry, and fine clothing into sacks.

As the sun lowered, Uri and his teen son slaughtered a young sheep and prepared it for cooking. The boy caught the lamb's blood in a bowl, and heavy dread filled my chest, crowding out the denial.

This wasn't some ancient myth.

The tenth plague was coming.

Tonight.

Uri's wife brought a handful of herbs, and Uri dipped them in the blood then painted it on the doorposts and lintel. He saw me watching and beckoned for me to climb down from the roof. I obeyed.

He draped his arm around my battered shoulders and led me inside the house. His urgent words meant nothing, but I understood when he gestured downward in the universal sign for "stay."

As he walked back outside, I brushed at wetness on my arm.

The streak of blood on my hand made me shiver. According to my mother's stories, every firstborn son in the region without lamb's blood around his door would die this night.

I was a firstborn son.

But I wasn't from this time. Would I really be safe inside Uri's home?

Did I want to risk death to find out?

I don't believe in gods. I believe in science.

But I couldn't deny all I'd seen, and bone-deep fear stripped my heart as bare as my feet.

I glanced out the door at Uri and his family one last time.

Then I ducked deeper into the house and escaped to my own time.

Back in my Luna apartment, I showered away blood and dirt, watching the pink water slowly swirl around the drain in the light gravity. I donned my usual clothing over tanned skin and pulled reassuringly sturdy boots onto socked feet.

I busied myself in lab research while my mind and body healed. Eventually, I was able to go barefoot without having flashbacks to stepping on frogs.

But the memory of shimmering hailstones melting under the Goshen sun remained lodged in my exposed heart and refused to dim with time.

FIRST-TIME DRIVER

Elizabeth Anne Myrick

"Oh no! Oh no! Nixie, what have I done?" Jope yanked his hands away from the control panel. Lights blinked along the dash, but he pressed fists to his eyes and leaned his weight against the harness. He couldn't bear to look at the teleportation platform across the cabin. It was ominously, horribly silent.

"Don't touch anything," Nixie hissed. Her hands flew over the controls, and the ship hummed in response.

"I'm not touching anything!"

"Why are you yelling at me? Stop yelling!"

"I'm not yelling!"

Nixie's harness groaned as she leaned forward, looking out the cockpit window. The desert at night was a sea of black, but two hundred feet below, fires glowed orange against the sand. "Jope, do you know what you've just done?"

Jope pulled his fists away from his eyes and glared at his sister. "No, Nixie. Please tell me exactly how badly I've messed up my very first abduction."

With a final *beep*, the ship quieted, and Nixie pushed away from the controls. Her neon blue hair had fallen from its ponytail and wisped across her quickly paling face. "Dad is going to kill us," she whispered.

In unison, Jope and Nixie turned to the teleportation platform and stared at the block of limestone.

Jope had prepared for this moment for years—his very first abduction. Nixie had helped plan the surprise, suggesting the Sahara as a prime location. His father had a soft spot for ancient Egypt, and Jope thought it would be a fun birthday present to get one of the pharaohs for his dad. It matched his name—Farro—after all.

Except it wasn't a pharaoh on the teleportation platform. It wasn't a scribe or a stone cutter or even a slave—and there were plenty of those. Instead, he'd abducted a piece of the *statue*.

Just a lump of rock. No screaming. No crying. No pounding against the glass partition. Jope dreaded telling his dad that, instead of a birthday present, this year he'd be getting an alternate time continuum for his favorite monument.

"Fix it." He turned to Nixie. "You have to put it back."

"Put it back?" She rolled her eyes. "This isn't one of those fancy hyperspace ships, Jope. It's just a patrol. It can't handle another teleportation for at least twenty-four hours."

Jope groaned. "At least say the cloaking device is working."

Controls clicked and beeped. "Yep. We still look like a cloud."

"So the locals shouldn't have noticed anything, right?"

"Except that a giant piece of limestone is missing? Sure. They didn't notice a thing."

Jope looked at the stone. He decided it was probably the statue's nose. "It's dark. No one will know what happened. We could just, you know, drop it."

Nixie was silent. She unstrapped her harness and walked to the platform. "I mean... it's not a wholly terrible idea."

"We've gotta be quick." Jope slipped out of his own harness and ran to the release button. "Before—"

The intercom beeped, and Jope wished he'd turned off the auto-answer feature. Static crackled, and then Farro's voice crackled overhead. "Jope? Nixie?"

"Hey, Dad!" Nixie said brightly. But the look she gave Jope was panicked. "What's up?"

More staticky silence, then, "I want you home in five minutes. We'll talk about this when you get here." The transmission cut out.

It would take twenty minutes to activate the drop chute, chuck the nose, and then recheck all the systems before warping home.

"Maybe he won't be that mad," Jope said. "He helped you put back that one author, right? And it didn't break the time continuum. So no one would notice if we just put it back in a couple days, right?"

"First of all"—Nixie shook her head—"Mom is the one who made me put her back. Apparently, that lady hadn't written, like, any of her famous books yet. Mom refused to lose Hercule Poirot to a faulty timeline, but people still noticed. She was missing for eleven days—and that was in the modern era. You just abducted a two-ton piece of limestone from hundreds of years before that. Maybe thousands. The amount of fuel that would take..." She shook her head. "The continuum's messed up already."

Jope hung his head while Nixie set the coordinates for home.

When the ship docked, Farro was waiting on the platform. He stormed into the ship before the doors had even fully opened.

"What were you thinking?" he fumed, rounding on Nixie first. "He got his license two days ago, and you think it's a good idea to take him gallivanting across the centuries?"

"It was my idea," Jope said. "I wanted to surprise you. Um. Happy birthday!" He motioned to the teleporter.

When Farro saw the limestone nose, he froze. "Is that..." He cleared his throat. "From the Sphinx?"

"Okay, I'm sorry," Jope blurted. "I think it was the settings. I was trying for one of those old pharaohs—the forgotten ones, of course, 'cause I know better than to mess with people we still remember—but I'm pretty sure I bumped it to non-biological. And the guy was right under the nose when I aimed, and... and..." He stopped.

Farro was laughing.

"Um, Dad?" Nixie pushed her blue hair out of her face. "Are you okay?"

"Let's add it to the collection." With a grin, Farro led Jope and Nixie out of the ship.

They exited the port, followed him into a waiting hovercraft, and sped along the road. But they didn't go home. Instead, Farro drove into one of the many storage units built into the mountain caves. Inside, lights and voices met them. Jope gaped.

A sprawling ancient city filled the space. Pristine marble columns, bubbling fountains, and even people, milling about as if everything was completely normal.

"Welcome to Atlantis," said Farro. "My own accidental-abduction. Now, Jope. I think the Sphinx's nose would look lovely displayed in the temple."

REGINALD'S SATURDAY MORNING SURPRISE

Rachael Watson

"Reginald!"

At ten years old, I was well-versed in my mother's acoustic range and recognized this dangerous pitch. I peered out from under my covers—the clock announced "8:00 a.m." in bright red. On a Saturday morning. Why was I already in trouble?

Panic pulsated through me. I sprang out of bed, landed with two feet solidly on the hardwood floor, and raised my hand in a crisp salute. Mother opened the door. At sight of my soldierly pose, indignant anger brewed in her eyes. I yanked my hand back down.

"Reginald? What do you have to say for yourself?" Mother had been in the kitchen; I could tell by her orange flowered apron and the smell of burnt pancakes that wafted in with her.

"Is this about the tadpoles?" I'd offered tadpoles refuge in our fridge from the unseasonable heat yesterday, to avoid a boiled catastrophe. It had required emptying out the pickles to find a suitable jar, but no one ate pickles in our family anyway.

"Tadpoles? No, it's about *that*." Raising her spatula, with crispy burnt pancake bits clinging to it, she pointed behind me.

I turned my head, clearing the sleep from my eyes. The top of a massive wooden object loomed outside my half-open window, framed by rippling white curtains. It was a horse. Its nose filled my window, giant twin nostrils resting on the ledge.

"Oh, that." Not the tadpoles.

"How do you explain it?" Her strained voice warbled.

"Expertly crafted. Approximately the height of a two-story house, solid wood, perhaps built to imitate an animal of the equestrian family." I strove to be factual.

"I can see all that, Reggie. How did it get into our backyard? On today of all days, too!"

"I cannot say how it arrived. Wait, what is happening today?" Anything but Aunt Gladys visiting with her pungent perfume.

"Your father's university coworkers are coming over—the entire philosophy department!" It occurred to me that they were probably better qualified to argue the origins of the particular species in our backyard than I was, but I chose not to share that opinion.

"For breakfast?" I tried to divert her thoughts from the massive lawn ornament.

"Brunch!"

"Brunch? Why not dinner?" An honest inquiry, I was truly perplexed.

"Who knows with these academics, Reginald? You have exactly fifty-five minutes to get rid of that." She wiggled her spatula toward the horse, then slammed the door shut.

I frantically ran to the window and shoved it fully open. Large, beady glass eyes stared at me from their perch at the top of the enormous nose. This was not the weekend mischief I had anticipated.

The detail on this wooden specimen was impressive. The

horse even had a flowing chestnut mane. I clambered out the window, knobby knees and elbows catching on the harsh edges, and launched myself onto the apparatus, landing smack between its eyes. Scrambling up the forehead and down the neck, I settled on the broad space of its back.

Next door, my neighbor Carlos leaned out of his bedroom window. His eyes bugged out at the sight of me on my steed. I waved, and he quickly retreated inside, shutting his window.

"Fifty minutes, Reginald!" My mother yelled from the kitchen window, fanning smoke from the charred bacon.

I carefully inspected my ride for any clue regarding its purpose. On the right hindquarter, I saw **Epeius** expertly carved. Sounded Greek to me. Perhaps the maker?

Inspired by the hollow wooden horse myth, I decided to knock.

Knock, knock, knock.

Pigeons cooed mockingly from our fence.

Knock, knock, knock.

My knuckles smarted.

The word **Epeius** creakily lifted into the air, and a man, diminutive in stature, peered out from a hidden hatch.

"Yes?" His accent was thick, and he appeared dressed for battle, wearing a bronze helmet with a red plume waving in the breeze.

"Good morning. May I ask what you're doing here?"

"We're a gift for you!" A second man enthusiastically popped up beside the first, helmet askew. "Happy Birthday!"

"It's not my birthday." I blinked.

The first man shoved his unhelpful comrade back down the hatch. "Sir, where are we?" He lifted his chin confidently, but I saw confusion in his eyes.

"North America." I decided any more particulars wouldn't be helpful. He looked around, a deep furrow forming in his brow.

"Could you direct us towards Troy?" he inquired over loud whispers from inside the horse.

"REGGIE! They're all early!" Mother frantically bellowed from the patio door. She wouldn't be able to see the Greek from her angle. Regardless, time was up. I could not easily manipulate the clock or this wheeled monstrosity full of confused ancients.

The Greek leaned forward. "Your commanding officer?"

"Worse, my mother, and she is not pleased."

"Did you lose her goats?" The second Greek had escaped from below again.

"I'm ruining a breakfast party with important guests." I put my head in my hands. Hopefully none of the guests wanted pickles.

"A gathering at breakfast?" The first soldier frowned in dismay. His compatriot seemed equally appalled.

"Academics." I shrugged, and they nodded empathetically. Their sympathy presented an opportunity, and I abruptly decided to seize it. "Men of courage, I require your assistance. Provide it, and I pledge to find a way to return you to Troy."

The two Greeks put their helmets together and privately consulted. I glanced down, checking for stray professors.

"We will help." The first man solemnly placed his hand over his breastplate.

"Yes, but what should be done about your mother's goats?" the second man chirped.

My mind whirred, a solution forming. It required curtains.

That is how my mother came to have a performance of Homer's *Iliad* featuring myself, my curtains, and thirty ancient Grecians as brunch entertainment. The academics marveled at the actors' impeccable costuming and enthusiastic depiction of Troy's demise. To my great relief, no one asked for pickles.

Eventually, the horse was gifted to the correct recipients.

MISS KOBE

Kevin King

Nadia had slept three nights in the house she'd inherited from her grandmother, and every night, she had the same dream. Nightmare, really. She heard crying coming from the attic, and when she went to investigate, she found a three-foot-tall Japanese woman trapped in a wooden crate. Then the dream shifted, and *she* was trapped in a crate. She cried and cried, but nobody let her out.

Remnants of the dream clung to the edges of Nadia's brain like cobwebs. She shuffled into the bathroom and splashed water on her face, trying to wash them away. The old pipes groaned. For a moment, their vibration sounded almost like crying.

She shut off the water. Chilly droplets trickled down her face, dripping into the sink. The tinnitus that she'd developed in her thirties masked sounds in a certain frequency. She could almost make out a faint... something. But not quite.

Images of a crate flashed in her mind randomly as she brushed her teeth.

Her eggs nearly burned as she stood, a greasy spatula hanging from her right hand, listening for cries. They rang in her head. But were they real? The smell of singed butter brought her back to herself. Her fingers trembled as she shut off the gas burner.

"This is crazy. I have to check," Nadia muttered, pinching the bridge of her nose with her left hand. Her right hand tightened on the spatula. She carried it with her as she made her way to the hall and pulled down the attic stairs. It felt a bit nuts, wielding a greasy spatula as if it were an effective weapon against anything bigger than a spider.

Then again, here she was climbing into the attic looking for a three-foot-tall woman in a crate that she'd seen in a dream. Carrying a spatula ranked pretty far down this morning's weirdness list.

The attic smelled of must and decay. Ominous shapes loomed in the darkness, a menagerie of blocky specters cloaked in shadow. Nadia fumbled, left-handed, for the chain to turn on the light. She yanked it hard enough to shower herself with dust and strands of fiberglass insulation. She swished the spatula back and forth, ready to fend off any threats.

Crumpled cardboard boxes formed precarious towers, piled three or four high in some places. Stacks of moth-eaten blankets, chairs with busted seats or broken legs, and an old sewing mannequin made up the random shapes that had felt so sinister in the dark. Nadia counted her breaths, in and out.

A wooden crate stuck out from behind a pile of boxes. Nadia's heart rate doubled.

"It's nothing, Nadia. Coincidence. You probably saw this as a child and the memory surfaced in your dreams." Her gut ignored her pep talk, refusing to unclench. She forced her trembling legs to carry her to the crate. She knelt and tried the lid.

Nailed shut.

She wedged the spatula beneath the edge, but only managed to bend the flimsy utensil.

Glancing around the attic, she spotted a rusty claw hammer. She pulled the thin nails loose with a wailing screech and lifted the lid. A three-foot-tall woman in traditional Japanese robes stared up at her from inside the crate. Shock froze Nadia in place.

It's a doll. The rational part of Nadia's mind wrestled with her primal instincts, gradually reasserting control. *It's not a woman. It's a doll. A doll can't hurt you.*

Shoulder-length black hair framed the doll's pale face. Its flat eyes looked dead, yet oddly alive.

This is bad. I should close it up and leave it.

Its faint smile radiated warmth and friendship. Nadia didn't want to trust it. But somehow, she did. Before she knew what she was doing, she reached out to pick it up. "Well, I can't just leave you here. Come on, I'll make us some tea while I decide what to do with you."

Tea for a doll? You really are going crazy. But I definitely need something hot and caffeinated for myself.

Twenty minutes later, the doll rested on a dining room chair while Nadia sat across from it, waiting for her tea to cool. As she looked into those painted eyes, her shoulders relaxed. Time stretched and lost all meaning. Something in the back of her mind struggled and cried out, but she closed a lid over it.

Why was I ever worried? She sat across from a friend, come to visit from far away.

"I'm sorry. It was rude of me to not offer tea to my guest. Would you like some?" Nadia hurried to make another cup. She set it in front of the woman. No. The doll. The woman. Dizziness swept over her. Foreign thoughts swirled in her head, not quite understandable. A name. "Is there anything else I can get for you, Miss Kobe?"

Whispers. Murmurings. Images of other crates and boxes, in unrecognizable storerooms and closets. Each of them crying. Then, out of the chaos, words formed.

Find... sisters. Free us.

"Yes, of course." Nadia reached across to take Miss Kobe's hand. "It's shameful how you've been treated. I'll do whatever I can to make it right. Help me find our sisters, and I will set them free. I promise."

X

THE SWORD STILL WITHIN THE STONE

EDITORS' CHOICE AWARD WINNER
S. M. Jake

Torryn's stomach tightened under their stares, and he flexed his grip on the ancient hilt. The sword's flat steel lay cold against his shoulder, overly heavy in both weight and responsibility.

"That's..." The old man at the center of the table shook his head, the glittering jewels and embroidery attesting to how much he and the other lords had "suffered" under this war. "That's not what the legend speaks of."

Torryn's jaw clenched, his grandfather's ragged voice echoing in his head.

That bull-headed boy...

"Surely, this is jest." The lord from Torryn's province huffed, his brocade oversleeves tangling as he crossed his arms.

A willowy lord to the left pounded the table. "The true king will *pull* the sword from the stone! That is how we will know!"

"Indeed!" others chimed.

"Pretty sure..." Torryn drawled, shifting his weight casually to hide his nervous trembles. "The exact wording is 'wield the sword.' Not pull."

He swung the sword off his shoulder; the massive chunk of chiseled rock still adhered to the blade thunked onto the battered wood floor. He clenched the hilt with both hands, widening his stance. "I'm wielding it."

Voices echoed through the Great Hall as the lords dissolved into squabbles, sending servants skittering as they called for texts and records.

Around the edges of the room, knights stood watching, whispering and shrugging as they eyed Torryn. They obviously knew the horrors this war had wrought. They wore grime of endless battles in every crevice of their armor, bore the strikes of the enemy in each dent and broken link of mail, carried the ghosts of loss and the guilt of hard choices within their eyes. Yet none of that meant they would follow him.

Torryn was far from kingly. He was big—all feet and hands, stature, and waist. Thick through the middle and through the head, barely able to read and no mind for numbers. For all his strength and willingness to work, he had yet to outgrow the clumsiness of adolescence. And acne had set in with a vengeance, riddling his plain face with painful welts. Torryn was a nobody and looked the part.

That bull-headed boy...

He forced his hands to loosen, blisters screaming across his palms and fingers. It'd taken him two weeks to chisel the rock. He'd thought to strip it clean, but the closer he got to the blade, the harder the rock grew, clinging with a ferocity that became impenetrable. But Torryn wasn't picky, so, he'd settled for something else.

He'd turned a sword into a hammer. One that only he had the bull-headed notion to attempt to swing.

"It's too poetic!" the gem-crusted lord railed as he threw aside another scroll into the growing pile behind him. "Completely untrustworthy! Find another!"

Voices rose higher, the leaders of the land hunching farther over their table now covered in parchments and books.

Metal flashed, catching Torryn's eye as a knight stepped forward. Gray flecked his trim beard, each step brimming with confidence and strength as he crossed to the center of the room and stopped in front of Torryn.

"You know who I am, boy?" His voice was quieter than Torryn expected, but it held a weightiness that blanketed the room. A scar cut through the thick eyebrow which rose with the knight's skeptical glare. The lords grew quiet behind him.

A green surcoat with a silver stallion. This man came from Torryn's province, but who? His mind came up blank.

"No," Torryn said.

The brow arched higher. Knights whispered. His stony gaze dropped, eyes narrowing as he seemed to take in Torryn's mangled handiwork. "Did you try to pull it?"

"Yes."

The knight nodded, waving down the half-buried blade. "And when it didn't work, you did this. Turned the sacred sword into a brutish hammer."

Torryn forced air into his nerve-strangled chest. "Yes."

"Why?"

His stomach lurched, but he wouldn't shy from the truth. Even if the lords took his head for speaking it.

"'Cuz my parents' crops were burned for the third year in a row, and tribute is still demanded." Saying it aloud bolstered him, strengthening his voice and smoothing its tremble. "'Cuz raids from the enemy—and commandeered goods from our own— mean my village hasn't seen a trade caravan in eight months, and our medicine ran out six past. 'Cuz my brother—"

His throat wrenched shut, blocking the words. He attempted

to go on, but it wouldn't budge. He flexed his shoulders and firmed his barely stubble-lined jaw, blinking quickly as he fought to hold the man's gaze. His voice came back, softer, but no less determined. "I will see the war ended, and our people taken care of."

Murmuring traced down the lords' table, scowls deepening. Knights shifted along the edges of the room but held their silence as they watched the man in green.

A smirk tipped the green knight's mouth, his eyes growing dark with either spite or mischief. Perhaps both.

"Stubborn young man," he whispered, so softly Torryn was certain the words were meant for him alone.

And then he dropped to one knee.

Metal crashed as the green knight's fist rapped against his plated chest. "Long live the king!"

The room filled with the ring of metal, armor hitting the floor.

Torryn's head spun as knights of every banner fell to their knees, beating their breastplates and taking up the chant. The servants behind followed suit, while the lords screamed in fury.

Could he really do this? Take hold of the throne that had been vacant so long? Lead a kingdom? End a war? That had been his plan. Yet now, staring it in the face, his nerves faltered, fear creeping in. He was no king. He was barely even a man.

His grandfather's words cut through the chaos, interweaving determination with the fear, and firming his grip on the ancient hilt.

That bull-headed boy... Too stubborn to let go of hope. Too stiff-necked to give up on us.

HER REGULAR

Sophia L. Hansen

"Mocha. Half-pump. Extra hot. Whipped cream."

"What size?" she asked without her voice trembling. Almost.

It would be Medium—always was. But... to hear him speak again... she could live with sounding stupid.

"Medium."

The three syllables dripped from his lips with just a hint of a sigh, almost compensating for the fact that he barely looked up from his phone.

"Name?" She hoped her smile wasn't too eager.

"Rupert."

"Rupert," she croaked. Somehow, she managed to scribe the perfect name on white cardboard without adding a heart underneath. Then, she turned to hide her shaking hands while she fixed his order.

How did this happen? He wasn't even a prince. *Why isn't he a prince?*

Her shoulders drooped. She was supposed to kiss a prince. The naiad's prophecy said love waited for her under the crown, and the first crown she saw upon emerging into this world hung over the coffee shop door.

But there'd been no prince. No hint of any magic. Just the daily grind, with one bright spot each afternoon, who made her curse almost bearable.

No. That wasn't quite true—Rupert was much more than bearable. Her afternoon regular had transformed this land-locked imprisonment into a bubble of hope.

She held his mocha just out of reach, forcing him to look up to claim it. Her gaze lifted from the dark fingers wrapping around the cup to his impossibly deep green eyes. A shiver tripped down her spine. Their fingers brushed, and a shiver of joy broke free.

His slight hop back, however, deflated her. She looked away to hide her disappointment.

I repulse him.

Biting her lip to fight the welling tears, she steeled herself and turned to the next customer.

I repulse her.

Rupert's attention dropped down to his blank phone.

Every day he visited her coffee shop.

Every day she asked for his name.

She never remembered his order, though it never varied.

Does she even know I exist?

That brief touch and her shudder revealed what he'd feared: he had no chance with a beauty like her.

If only they'd met in his homeland. There, she might have been impressed, like the swarms of females that'd followed him.

Here, he was nobody. A nothing. Hope melted with the whipped cream in his coffee.

But the Fates had drawn him here, divested him of everything he'd had and everything he'd known, far from his secluded kingdom. He was bound to follow this path—or perish in the attempt.

If only she could be the one...

He would have liked to learn her name, at least.

Rupert studied the dregs of his coffee with a sigh. Tomorrow brought another sun. He'd try again. Perhaps the next day's froth and foam would reveal a new portent.

Phoebe fought anticipation as the sun meandered across the sky and the shadows stretched. Soon her regular would arrive.

This first herald before evening had always been her favorite time of day—when friends and family gathered to feast and sing. But it had been ages since she'd joined her community's nightsong.

She held the air in her lungs—eyes closed—then released both wish and breath.

A clearing throat broke the reverie. She blinked as her daydream morphed into flesh.

"Mocha. Half-pump. Extra hot. Whipped cream."

"Medium?" she dared ask.

Green eyes flashed up to meet hers. "Y-Yes." His voice cracked.

Was it the change in their script? She risked again, marker poised above the cup. "Rupert?"

"You know..." His cheeks flushed. "You know my name?"

She nodded, lips pressed tight.

"Do you... have ... a name?" His gaze dropped to his feet. "Dumb," he muttered.

"Actually"—she reached across the counter and touched his wrist—"it's Phoebe."

"Ph-Ph-Phoebe? It's a pleasure... to meet—Well, I suppose we've already met."

A chuckle burbled up, but this time Phoebe didn't suppress it.

"Yes, we have."

"Phoebe," Rupert breathed her name. "Would you... Could we... take a walk?"

Her smile leapt from her face to her heart. "That would be lovely."

....

They walked and talked throughout the evening. Then the next evening. And the next.

"Dusk is my favorite time of the day," Phoebe divulged. "It's always been."

"Mine as well." Rupert covered her hand with his. "And your company makes it sweeter."

"*Mmm.*" These twilight walks filled Phoebe with joy. Though she missed her former life and wondered if she could fully acclimate to this world, far from home, her heart whispered that she wouldn't be alone.

"Phoebe." Rupert stopped before the pond they both enjoyed visiting. "I would very much like to..." He traced her temple, lingering on the tendrils framing her face. "What I mean to say is, may I kiss you?"

This was it. The choice was upon her. But in truth, she had none. Her first kiss *would* have broken the curse, but her heart had chosen a man, not a prince.

Phoebe turned her face up, forsaking kingdom, future, and family as his lips pressed against hers. Warmth cascaded through every part of her being, transforming any lingering doubt into joy.

She leaned back, eyes wide, as a cloud of green bubbles swirled around them.

Fear seized her. "What's happening?! I feel..." She clutched Rupert.

"I don't know." His voice deepened in the whirling bubbles. "Or maybe, I do."

Phoebe looked at him, and then at her hands. She was shrinking into her former self. "The curse—it's broken! But how?"

"You were spelled, too?" Rupert's disbelief showed plainly.

"Yes! But only a prince's kiss could break that spe—Oh." He was shrinking, too. "Your Majesty!" Phoebe bobbed in her most practiced amphibian bow.

The two frogs stared, blinking at the other's transformation, and their own.

"The Fates' froth and foam proved true," Rupert croaked with gleaming eyes. "You need not bow before me, sweet Phoebe. You gave me your heart when I was a nobody."

"You were never a nobody to me. You were my regular."

PEACE

Hannah Carter

You can't eat morals. This motto had earned Abraham quite the reputation across town, meaning many shady characters ended up in his tent on darkened nights. When the work Abraham had done for his clients tormented his mind, he told himself one thing.

Scruples didn't stave off starvation—money did.

And the fellow in front of him held a bag full of it, enough to feed Abraham for weeks.

Abraham shifted forward, his legs crossed as he sat on the floor. "So all I need to do is find this pregnant woman and kill her."

The stranger, swathed in amaranthine-colored clothes and jewels, reclined against a cushion. He toyed with a silver coin, staring at Abraham with dark, hooded eyes. "Precisely. A *teenage* girl, need I remind you. Barely grown. A man like yourself should have no problem taking care of my... *issue*. Not to mention the location is ideal—a stable on the outside of town."

Abraham imagined the face of a girl his sister's age and winced. *No—stop.* He didn't care who this teenage girl was—a jilted lover, a disobedient daughter, an unfaithful wife. And he certainly was in no position to judge an adult man who wanted her dead, either. This stranger might have been paying for the knife, but Abraham was the one who would drive it through her heart. "All right. What do you want as proof that the job is done?"

A thin smile curved the man's lips. "Oh, I'll have ways of knowing when she's dead." He tossed the bag of thirty coins to Abraham, and a few spilled onto the ground. The stranger's voice turned prickly, like thorns in a garden. "But if you break our agreement, I'll have you arrested and crucified for all your sins."

Abraham stuffed the fallen silver pieces back into the leather bag. "I'll do it tonight."

Abraham hated crowds, and right now the town bustled with people due to the census. Crowds typically meant witnesses, which made Abraham's work harder. But he could also use it to his advantage. No one would notice if a slip of a girl and her unwanted baby went missing. Every relative would just assume she was with someone else until they realized the truth. Even then, they may not suspect her dead.

He coughed, an attempt to loosen the lump in his throat.

I've killed before. Lots of times. Never cared before if they were guilty or innocent.

Another strangled cough.

It's one more person's blood on my hands. Who they are doesn't matter.

Sand collected on Abraham's sandals as he followed the man's instructions to a stable on the outskirts of town. A star blazed brightly overhead, illuminating the path before him.

His grip tightened on his knife as he neared. No sound drifted from the large house up on the hill, the closest residence. All the candles had been blown out for the night.

Something snapped in the bushes behind him.

He whirled around and threw the knife at the sound with

practiced accuracy. Whatever lurked there died with a quiet bleat, and Abraham raced over to find—

A lamb.

Cursing his nerves, he yanked the knife out of the lamb's side. Some shepherd would be punished for that, surely. And if it somehow got traced back to Abraham...

No, impossible. It was one sheep. In a huge flock, would one even be noticed?

Abraham swallowed, though the action felt like he'd stabbed himself in the esophagus. He hacked and wiped his mouth, but the pain didn't lessen.

One stupid sheep. One stupid teenage girl. One stupid lump in his throat choking him.

He wanted this job to be *over*.

The barn was a few yards away now. He crept toward it, muscles tense. The star in the sky seemed to burn brighter, like a second, watchful moon with its eye on him.

A girl's cry shattered his nerves.

No! She couldn't give birth now. That would draw attention. Someone might come check—

He dashed to the stable, but by the time he got there, a second wail joined the first. Knife poised for the kill, Abraham burst inside, his only thought to silence the mother and newborn. But instead, he dropped to his knees.

The girl lay on a bedroll, propped up on hay. A man crouched beside her, his arm around her shoulders, one hand protectively placed against an infant. And the baby himself...

The emotional dam that had strangled Abraham all night exploded as he glimpsed the infant's face. There was nothing extraordinary about the child—the babe was quite plain, covered in afterbirth—but when he turned his eyes upon Abraham, the rest of the world faded away.

The babe's eyes had only opened for a second, seeing the world for the first time. So how, when they met Abraham's, did they carry the weight of the world in them? How did they pierce him from across the stable, expose all the blood on his hands, and strew his sins across the room like the straw? But this newborn child carried no condemnation in his eyes.

Abraham's grip on his knife slipped, the blade still covered in the blood of the lamb.

Had he ever known peace until he'd seen those eyes?

"Who are you?" the man asked, his voice gruff, the reverent moment destroyed. He rose halfway to his feet, his face red. "What's your business here?"

"I—" Abraham fought to loosen his tongue.

The girl placed her hand against the man. She glanced knowingly at the knife before she offered Abraham a tired smile. "It's okay, Joseph. I think we'll have all sorts of visitors tonight." She adjusted the infant in her arms. "Would you like to come meet Yeshua?"

The glow of the star poured through the windows, shafts falling on the infant's head.

"Yes," Abraham whispered.

Peace.

Outside the stable, Abraham could have sworn he heard singing.

X

LEGENDARY PEOPLE

GROUNDED

Rachel Lawrence

I pedaled furiously, squinting to make out the next turn by the beam of the flashlight tucked into my bike basket.

My mom would catch up with me soon, I was sure of it. Even if I hadn't left the shoebox of old newspaper clippings and my scribbled notes from library trips strewn across my bedspread, she would know where I'd gone.

It had been the source of most of our disagreements recently, ever since my history project turned into an obsession. What started as a simple poster board and an afternoon scrolling through microfilm had ended—or so Mom thought—with her forbidding me to leave my room outside of school hours. Her overreaction only fueled my curiosity and determination.

"I don't understand what is going on with you, Mary. The assignment was completed weeks ago. You've been skipping meals, neglecting your chores, ignoring your father and me. It's like you aren't even here. Why can't you let this go?"

"This was a major event, Mom!" I'd argued. "You're telling me she just disappeared, and they never found the plane or anything? And why was everyone so quick to give up? Someone knows something."

"Sweetheart, this was over forty years ago. A man has gone

to the moon. They're talking about computers being able to communicate with one another soon, right from inside people's homes. Everyone has moved on. Considering you weren't even alive then, maybe you should move on too."

But my heart drove me, *compelled* me, to press forward. There was something to this latest theory. It felt different. Close. As close as the jacket I wore now, the one from the thrift store with the small A.E. sewn inside the collar, the spark that had set this fire. I'd never experienced such a strong connection to a stranger, such a thirst for resolution.

I steered up close to the chain-link fence and dragged my foot. This was the third time I'd visited the large junkyard rumored to have pieces of an aircraft that possibly fit the description I'd read dozens of times. It would be easy to hide something in plain sight if no one was looking for it anywhere close to here.

I had just found a spot by a tree to start climbing the fence when headlights hit me. I groaned. If only I'd thought to conceal my bike!

But when my eyes adjusted, the figure exiting the driver's side wasn't my mother.

"Grandma?" I jogged over to meet her. "You aren't even supposed to be driving."

"Says the girl who's supposed to be in her bedroom right now," she replied. "Your mom is worried sick, you know."

Guilt washed over me. It would have been easier to stay angry if I was staring into Mom's eyes instead. "I know, Grandma. I just—"

"You just what? What are you doing out here at this hour, Mary?"

I opted for the truth. Everyone else already thought I was insane. "Looking for Amelia Earhart's plane."

Her melodic laugh echoed through the darkness, but it held

no hint of ridicule. "Here on the east coast? Honey, that plane was last seen far from here."

"Yes, but—" I bit my lip, weighing my next words. The way her eyes sparkled in the moonlight told me I could trust her. "But what if it wasn't?"

Grandma crossed her arms and nodded a go-ahead. The first person willing to listen to me.

"I've run across some things that make me wonder. What if she was never found because she never *wanted* to be found? She was always afraid she'd be pulled from what she loved by obligations or others' expectations of her. What if she disappeared so she could start over? And where better to go than Kitty Hawk, the birthplace of flight?"

She studied my face. "That's an interesting theory," she agreed. "And the one that always made the most sense to me."

I suddenly wished I'd sought her opinion on this long ago. She would have been about the same age as Ms. Earhart back then and, from what I knew of her personality, would have understood the struggles of the time for a woman with ambition.

"I just wonder," I continued, "if that was the case, how long did she keep flying? And why did no one ever recognize her?"

Grandma stepped closer. "A mystery indeed." She slid an arm around my shoulder. "My guess is she found a better adventure, something she learned to love even more than the beauty of weightless independence, something that still required every bit of her moxie and courage."

I didn't realize I was crying until she pulled a wrinkled tissue from her pocketbook.

"What's this really about?"

"I just thought…" I sniffled. "That if she ended up here, I'd have some kind of link to her. That this feeling I've always had that I was born for adventure would make sense. That maybe I could do daring things one day too."

She laughed again, this time through tears of her own. "Honey, you *were* born for adventure. But you don't need some old plane to prove that. You'll find adventure in the present, not the past. And in a future with the people who love you."

I leaned into her, and she wrapped me in a hug. "You're right, Grandma."

"Let's get you home."

I started to retrieve my bike but hovered by the fence. What *did* I really know about my grandma's past? "As long as we're here..." I shrugged. "We might as well check it out, right?"

She shook her head, but she grinned from ear to ear. "Your mother isn't going to let you leave your room for a long time after tonight, so we'd better make it count."

"Some things are worth being grounded for."

"Don't I know it, kid." She winked, her eyes lingering for a moment on my jacket. "Now, let's head around the back. There's a gap in the fence."

HADES FOR THE HOLIDAYS

Hailey Huntington

Some people think that the lord of the underworld is scared of nothing.

Those people have clearly never met my mother-in-law.

"You know, we could celebrate by ourselves this year. Just the two of us," I said as Persephone wrapped evergreen boughs around the Corinthian columns lining the courtyard. "It's not too late to change plans. I mean, Demeter hates it down here." Honestly, *hates* was probably an understatement.

"Hades, the holidays are meant to be spent with family. It is one day, and you will be fine." Dropping the evergreens, she rested her hands on my arms. "I'll try and keep Mother from being too… overbearing."

I was ready to argue back, but Sephone looked up at me with her gentle green eyes, and all my reasons dissolved. I was hopeless when it came to her. Zeus liked to tease me about acting like a lovesick teenager, but when a guy only gets to see his wife for half the year, he'll do anything to make her smile.

Even if it means suffering a day with Demeter.

"Now, why don't you go take Cerberus for a run while I finish decorating. Don't forget to kennel him when you get back," she added, a twinge of guilt crossing her face. My gargantuan dog and his antics were yet another one of my many faults in Demeter's eyes.

"Right. Don't want a repeat of Thanksgiving two years ago." I grimaced at the memory.

Sephone pressed a quick kiss to my cheek before gathering up her pine boughs again. "Thank you." Turning, she continued down the courtyard, leaving life and vibrancy in her wake.

I let out a deep sigh. For Sephone. I could do this for her.

And if things got too hard, I could always go hide with Cerberus in the doghouse. Demeter wouldn't go anywhere near those three heads after last time.

Cerberus drool dripped down my back as I walked through the villa. I needed to change. I'd successfully tired my affectionate hellhound enough to go into his kennel, but that meant I was also wiped. The massive dog had more energy than one of Zeus's lightning bolts.

A deep, ominous gong rang through the hallway—the doorbell. Wiping slobber off my forehead, I headed to the front door. Charon was probably dropping off the latest ferry reports and doubtlessly would talk about that raise he—

I froze when I opened the door. "Demeter."

Pursing her lips together, Demeter took in my sweat-and-spit-soaked shirt and muddy shoes. Her forehead pinched. "Hades." Her tone was flat. Without waiting for so much as a *"Come on in,"* or *"How have you been,"* Demeter swept past me, nose high in the air.

My fist curled around the door handle.

So it begins.

I'm mature enough to admit that I sulked over my ambrosia tea as Demeter and Sephone caught up with each other. The slights and jabs Demeter made toward me didn't escape my notice, but for Persephone's sake, I held back my retorts.

Things didn't improve when we made cookies. While dumping out the flour, I managed to send a plume of it up in the air, coating me in white. Sephone's golden laughter warmed me until I noticed Demeter's hard stare. Messes are unacceptable to Demeter the perfectionist.

When Sephone decided to pull out the board games while the cookies baked, I grinned. Hermes never believes me, but running the underworld requires a strategic and businesslike mind. And those qualities make me great at games.

Demeter, apparently, also has those qualities.

My scowl—which had become my permanent expression that day—deepened when I looked at my dice roll. I just *had* to land directly on my mother-in-law's property.

Demeter had the gall to smile at my misfortune. "I knew building all those villas would pay off."

A distant chime suddenly rang through the air.

"Oh! The cookies! Be right back." Sephone popped up, hurrying out of the room.

I tensed at being left alone with Demeter. I needed Sephone to act as mediator. A heavy, awkward silence fell.

After a long moment, Demeter folded her hands together. "Maybe I've been a little too harsh on you, Hades."

I blinked. Had a rogue lightning bolt hit me? Was I hallucinating?

"You make Persephone smile. You care for her. While I know that things aren't ideal—"

I snorted, interrupting her. Yeah, that was what the lord of the underworld got when he married the maiden of spring: *not ideal*.

Demeter cleared her throat, continuing. "I've realized that your affection isn't merely a passing phase. So I hope that the two of you are happy together. And maybe things will change someday."

I rubbed the back of my neck. "Umm. Thanks." Was that the closest I was going to get to Demeter saying she approved of me? There must have been something strange in the air. Or maybe there was some stock in all of the rumors about the holidays being a magical time...

"Who wants a fresh cookie?" Sephone stepped into the room holding a tray high. I snatched a still-warm gingerbread scythe and popped it into my mouth.

Demeter was all business again. "Now, I believe that you still owe me for landing on my vineyard, Hades. Two thousand drachma, if my math is correct."

Or maybe there wasn't some weird magic. But Sephone might have had a point about holidays being spent with family—even mothers-in-law.

A PEACE OF THE STARS

Victoria Roberts

July 4th, 2050

I didn't think my husband and I would qualify for the program. Things don't usually go our way, especially since Gavin's release from active duty and the months of trauma that followed. He sits next to me, his fingers playing with his ID badge. The word ARMY is emblazoned across it. Reaching into the glove compartment, I retrieve my military spouse badge and a wrinkled sheet of paper that I slip onto his lap. His fingers still. His brow furrows as he looks at the crayon wishes we wrote as seven-year-olds. At the top of each list is the misspelled word ASTRONOT.

"You kept this?" he asks.

"Of course. It's how I knew we were soulmates."

He frowns, holding up the badge. "Not what you signed up for, huh?"

"It wouldn't be an adventure if we knew all the details now, would it?" I squeeze his hand. "Let's go."

I open the car door. Vehicles travel the road behind us heading toward the local Independence Day celebration. Distant explosions from early fireworks make Gavin jump, dropping his badge.

"Stella, wait." Gavin's grip on my hand tightens, tugging me back. "We should rethink this."

"We already have. A million times." I reach over, running my thumb across his freshly-shaved chin. "It's time to take the leap."

He exhales through gritted teeth. Hands shaking, he folds the drawing and slips it into his breast pocket before exiting the car. I retrieve his badge and meet him on the other side. Hand in hand, we walk into the newest NASA launch center.

Upon entering, we're greeted by an employee who scans our badges. He offers Gavin a handshake, expressing gratitude for his service. Gavin shakes his head, moving past me into the building. With a sigh, I step back to thank the employee before following. Program families fill the center with IDs representing different branches of the military. Above us, the gentle voice that coached us through space training speaks over the intercom.

"Welcome to PTSIS, the first space program fully committed to helping our combat heroes navigate post traumatic and transition stress through low impact space travel. Our inaugural Independence Day launch, Mission Spacious Skies, will begin shortly. Please proceed to your designated pods."

Gavin and I follow the route we memorized during space prep. This time, we'll actually enter our twenty-four-hour living pod for takeoff. My fingers tremble as I swipe my badge across the pod's scanner. The sliding panel door whirs open, allowing us entrance into the place I hope will begin to mend us.

Two launch chairs are set up on our left across from a roomy living space. Warm lights panel the ceiling and framed potted plants adorn the walls. A viewing window takes up the other half of the pod with a projection of the American flag on the pane.

I grin at Gavin. "Pretty cool, huh?"

He steps to the viewing pane, squinting at the projected flag.

"Dreams look different when you're older."

"We can get space suits if you really want some."

He grimaces, sweat beading his brow.

I reach up, taking his face between my hands. "We're going to be fine. We're in this together."

"I never wanted *this* for you."

I reach up, kissing the tip of his nose. "I've only ever wanted you."

"Mission Spacious Skies is about to commence. Please prepare for takeoff."

"Here we go."

I tug Gavin toward our launch chairs, helping him strap into his seat before slipping into mine. The lights around us dim as the pod begins to purr. The flag in the window disappears and we begin our ascent. As promised by NASA, a special impact shield protects us from the jarring launch typical of other rockets. The only indications of leaving the atmosphere are my sinking stomach and the world whizzing past the window. Ten minutes later, the pod stills as the voice of our space coach fills the room.

"Mission Spacious Skies has connected to the onboarding capsule. Enjoy your night in the stars. Thank you for your service."

For a moment, we sit breathless in our seats. Then, I activate the room's gravity button and unbuckle my straps. Gavin follows. I rush toward the viewing panel, gasping as Gavin joins me. Stars pepper the sky with a million pinpricks of light, blinking their welcome in a beautiful symphony. Below us, Earth floats close enough to see but far from the chaos that brought Gavin to his breaking point last year.

I glance out the side of the window where dozens of military families peek out of their pods to this new view of their country that, tonight, is rocked by celebratory noise and lights. Military heroes whose nerves are usually frayed by the explosions relax against an embrace of peace. A young boy in the pod next to us grins at me. When he catches Gavin's gaze, he offers him a salute.

Gavin clenches his fist once, twice. Then slowly, he returns the salute. My breath catches. He's refused to acknowledge any honor shown to him since his medical release. I blink back tears as he turns the salute toward the boy's mother, who wears a Navy badge. She reciprocates then turns to the service member in the next pod. One by one, across the reflective pods, the brightest stars in the galaxy exchange greetings of honor.

"Now this is a celebration," Gavin whispers.

He intertwines his fingers with mine.

I lean into his side. "You see? We *were* meant to be astronauts."

He laughs then. A full-throated laugh that makes my heart skip a beat. I thought life had stolen his laughter forever. Letting my tears fall, I lay my head against his shoulder. No fireworks display in the world stands a chance against this night. Someday we'll learn to endure the noise with our feet firmly planted on Earth. For now, we celebrate in peace among the stars, holding each other tight, while freedom rings below.

LEGENDARY

THE PATH TO THE SEA

Mia Rumi

Icarus was falling.
Foolish boy.
Daedalus had watched as his son soared toward the sun against his warning. For a moment, Icarus had been silhouetted against the gold brilliance, wings outstretched, an almost-Apollo.

But a moment later, seven feathers had already slipped from his son's makeshift wings, one sticking to Daedalus's cheek with quickly cooling beeswax. Its metallic iciness stung as if the feather had gone much deeper than the surface of his skin.

Icarus had faltered, his likeness to the sun god disintegrating in an instant. He flapped his wings, but, as such an action is the worst way to put out a fire, this only caused more feathers to dislodge from the wooden frames tied to his arms.

"Icarus, stop!" Daedalus had cried too late.

His son plummeted.

....

The sea rushed closer, a slate of sapphire webbed with ivory. Feathers of copper and bronze and hammered brass, sticky with thickening wax, clung to Icarus's back, his biceps, his cheeks. Salty mist kissed his face, strangely gentle, like a nurse attempting to ease the pain of what is to come.

He felt suddenly foolish with his flimsy wooden wings and clumsy metal feathers plastered to his skin, a little boy dirty from making crafts. But if he were a little boy, the worst he would get was a reprimand from his mother.

Though Icarus's path to the sea should have taken him seconds to traverse, it seemed an eternity. Perhaps Chronos had glanced over at his pitiable state, momentarily distracted from his eternal task of turning the wheel of time.

In that eerily long moment as he spiraled toward the water, Icarus's mind slipped from terror into a memory of a game he used to play with his friends by the cliff overlooking the sea. They would challenge each other to sprint toward the edge of the cliff, to get as close as they could without backing down. Once, at dusk in late spring, Icarus had competed with a boy who was nearly as daring as he. The boy ran farther than any other boy had gone without relenting. It was only when they had been several horse's paces away from the edge that the boy had surrendered and flung himself to the side. Icarus, caught by his momentum, might have kept going, but his brother, standing at the cliff edge to assess the game, had seized him around the middle and tackled him to the ground. They had lain in a panting heap on the dusty earth, Icarus's heart thudding in his ears like moth wings against a lantern.

"One day, I'm not going to be here to stop you," his brother had said.

And here he was now, spiraling toward the sea in a whirlwind of cold feathers and screaming wind.

"I'm sorry, Brother," Icarus thought—the wind pulled any words he might have said from his lips and carried them off somewhere he could not go. "I'm sorry, Father."

Daedalus soared toward his son, arm outstretched. But Icarus knew that if his father flew too close to the ocean, the sea mist would coat the feathers of his own makeshift wings and make them grow too heavy for flight. He knew because his father had told him.

In two swift movements, Icarus unfastened the straps holding his wrists to the wooden frames. He released his wings, now nearly devoid of feathers and unburdened by his weight, so that Daedalus had to swerve out of their path.

By the time Daedalus had steadied himself and re-emerged from a veil of clouds, his son was far out of reach, falling faster but somehow more gracefully without his wings.

Still, Daedalus dove toward the sea, but before his wings touched the mist blanketing its waters, it was too late.

Pearls of light glared up from the ocean's surface, children of the sun above—but it was not against gravity's will for Icarus to touch these. He was a minuscule figure in comparison to the sun, a mere speck of dust floating in its radiance. Glancing up, he saw an oblivious farmer plowing a field on a far-off coast just visible through the haze. And yet...

There was something quite beautiful about that. That idea that there was so much greater than him, that he could be a star in a sky that also housed the sun.

Somehow, just before the ocean came, he felt lighter, freer.

No one but perhaps Poseidon and a wandering hippocampus would know, but just before he hit the sapphire oblivion, Icarus smiled.

UNSINKABLE HEIRS

Morgan J. Manns

April 14, 1912
North Atlantic Ocean

"Isolde, listen to me!" My older brother's grip on my arm tightens as he pulls me toward the staircase. "The lifeboats are our only chance. This ship is sinking, and we both know it's not because of a blasted iceberg!"

I halt, making him turn. "Alaric, the passengers... They're going to die because of *us*."

His eyes, the same blue as the icy water rushing into this unsinkable ship, bore into my own. I think he's going to say I'm being absurd. Ridiculous, even. Instead, he pulls me into an embrace and says, "We had no choice."

The ship shudders and I muffle a sob. We did this. We brought doom upon the people of Earth.

He breathes out a long, low sigh as if he's read my thoughts. "I'm sorry my portal brought us here. It all happened so fast, I—"

"Don't apologize," I quickly say as a wave of painful memories resurfaces. After the assassins killed Mother and Father, we had to leave our world. "You got us here. You saved us." I won't let him feel this burden alone.

"But their wretched creatures followed." He growls out the words. "Maybe if we get to the lifeboats, we'll survive this attack, get away..." The lanterns on the wall flicker ominously as he tries to convince me that his cloaking shields will protect those with us. That we'll get them to safety. But I already know the plan won't work. That beast will continue chasing us, killing whoever gets in its way.

"No." I turn my chin upward, wiping away stray tears. "Enough running. We need to *fight*."

Alaric pauses before running a hand wearily down his face. "We can't. Our magic is unstable here. If we unleash our full power, we could burn out... It's too dangerous."

"We have to try anyways, for the people of Earth." I straighten, taking a step back. "They deserve our help."

I summon the slumbering power within me. Fiery heat erupts through my veins. It feels different, like slow-moving magma instead of a raging flame, but it doesn't matter. I feel *powerful*.

"Isolde..."

My consciousness widens. The agonized screams of passengers beyond the corridor pierce my psyche like daggers. I squeeze my eyes shut, seeking forgiveness as I block out their cries.

Steadying my breath, I guide my consciousness beyond myself. Below, I sense where unrelenting water floods through the breached hull. Studying the gaping hole, goose bumps rise upon my flesh. The beast that tore this ship open must be a hundred feet long.

Swallowing my fear, my essence drifts into the ocean waters. My heart jolts as I capture a glimpse of the dark serpentine creature. It circles like a shark, its jagged tail twirling behind.

It waits for our demise, but I vow to leave it disappointed. I'm the heir to the Golden Throne and I refuse to die.

"They've sent a *water dragon* after us?" Alaric bombards me with questions as we sprint toward the deck, and I recount what I've seen.

A deep groan resonates through the ship. I run faster, refusing to let fear paralyze me. If we fail at distracting the dragon, there's a good chance it will devour the lifeboats as they enter the water. I can't allow that to happen.

We emerge on the ship's deck, breathless. The canopy of stars blends into the glassy surface of the ocean. The disorienting illusion makes it appear we're adrift in the sky.

I'm brought back to reality as crew members frantically direct terrified passengers toward lifeboats. Knots form in my stomach as officers pull families apart, the men being left behind. There's not enough space for everyone.

I tear my eyes away, noticing the lifeboats. They remain suspended.

A kernel of hope blooms within my chest as I realize there's still time.

"Are you ready, Alaric?"

He presses his hands together and they flare golden.

Mother always told us I'm the sword and Alaric the shield—and together we're invincible. Tonight, I hope to honor her words.

We race to the stern, finding it deserted.

"I'll draw the dragon to the surface," I say, determined. "Then it's up to you."

He nods, stretching a hand above his head. A transparent dome ripples across the water. From it, an invisibility shield materializes, ensuring we remain concealed.

I concentrate on the ocean, glimpsing floating ice dotting the water's surface. My mouth turns up in a grin. That could be useful.

As I gather ice shards with my mind, it becomes apparent my power is dulled. Instead of the artful practice I'm used to, it feels like forcing opposite ends of a magnet together. The ice barely holds its weaponized shape.

Taking careful aim, I hurl the shaky ice spear toward the dragon. The weapon flies through the water like lightning and shatters against its side. It turns its head as if merely curious.

I collapse, and my consciousness slams back into my body.

The scales of a water dragon are impenetrable, but I now have its attention. My forehead aches as the cold night air shimmers around us. That took more energy than it should have.

"Did you hit it?" Alaric asks through clenched teeth. The light of his shield wavers. It won't last much longer.

"Yes, now get ready because—"

The obsidian-scaled beast erupts through the water's surface. With its fangs bared, it soars toward us, spiked tail whipping in its wake.

"Now!" I scream.

Maintaining his invisibility shield, Alaric extends his other hand.

My eyes widen as a colossal gateway materializes between us and the dragon, engulfing it. The portal swallows the beast whole, then winks out.

"Let's see how that oversized serpent fares in the Sahara Desert." Blood trickles from Alaric's nose as he slumps against the railing.

I merely nod, refocusing my attention on the lifeboats behind us. "Good, now let's help where we can."

The ship lurches, and I pray we aren't too late.

NOT TOO LATE

Andrew Winch

"You don't have to lie in that position, Vlad." I wasn't accustomed to making such intrusive suggestions to my patients, even ones who believed they were undead, but I wanted to make sure he knew this was a safe space. "It can't be comfortable."

"How do you mean, Doctor?" Eyes trained on the ceiling, arms across his chest, stiff as a board. Somehow, he'd succeeded in making my leather chaise lounge look like a coffin.

"Like... *that*. You're not here to convince me you're a vampire. You're here to begin healing." This was our third session, each after sundown per his request. *Not too late*, I'd insisted, as violent crimes were getting worse around here. But with the raging thunderstorm this evening, it *did* feel too late, and Valium could only do so much to calm my nerves.

He sighed, tapping a pointed fingernail on the bloodred handkerchief protruding from his midnight-black suit jacket. "But there is just the problem, Doctor. I *am* a vampire. An immortal creature of the night. With one such as I, how can there be healing?"

Finally, a moment of vulnerability! "Healing is just a form of change, Vlad. Nothing in this world stays the same." I leaned forward in my threadbare armchair. I'd found that patients opened up more when I presented myself humbly.

Lightning flared through my dimly lit office, and the corner of Vlad's curiously pale lips curled up. "Ah, yes. Change, like that antiquated chariot you drive. Once the height of modern engineering. Now, quite a... *humble* choice, no?"

I sat back. Surely a coincidence... "Do *you* find value in humility?"

His frown drew his cheeks impossibly thin. "Once, I surrounded myself with every opulence. Gold, silk, entertainment. Ah, the musicians and dancers and orators that filled my halls! But they all died away—either by the hand of time or my own. As you can imagine, I grew weary of replacing them. Even my brides eventually succumbed to cruel inevitability... Perhaps they were the lucky ones."

The ticking timepiece in his pocket grew louder, and in that tense moment, my heartbeat started to outpace it. I glanced at my desk drawer where my Valium waited. My finger twitched.

"Soon it was only the sound of my gramophone and my wearied steps filling the decaying emptiness of Castle Dracula."

Lightning flashed again, and my lights flickered. He was looking at me—neck turned at an impossible angle, teeth bared in a rictus grin, eyes utterly dark save for a faint reflection deep within. My breath caught. My hand crept toward my drawer. The lights flickered again, and he was staring up at the ceiling once more. I shook my head.

You're a doctor; get ahold of yourself! A deep breath slowed my heart. At our first meeting, I'd assumed a simple case of Renfield's Syndrome, and I'd written him a prescription for clozapine. By our second session, I realized that he didn't obsess over drinking blood. In fact, he rarely talked about it, and his delusions of grandeur seemed secondary as well. But as he'd paced the floor in my office like a caged predator, he did seem quite anxious, to the point of chronic insomnia. So, I'd prescribed him Valium, which I personally knew to be a lifesaver against the constant pressures of modern life. But now, as he reclined before me, speaking of days past and persistent regret, I cursed my brashness. This man was clearly depressed, forced into disassociation. I knew *just* the thing, and I pulled out my script pad.

As I set my pen to paper, a blinding flash preceded absolute darkness. Concussive thunder struck my chest. A long hiss swept across the room and slithered around behind me. My hand trembled as it moved to my desk drawer. Clinical anxiety scattered my thoughts. I needed to focus if I was to help my patient. I needed...

My fingers found the handle, slid the drawer open, gripped that comforting bottle, popped the cap.

"Can you imagine what it's like to be alive one second and dead the next, Doctor?"

The question floated out of the darkness like a dream. It tickled my right ear, but deep inside, impossible to scratch.

"It's not the dying that's painful. It's the return."

"I... I don't... Vlad, p-please return to your seat. This is quite inappropriate."

A cold, vicelike hand clutched my left shoulder, and a faint breeze played on my neck. "Ahh. You are a universal donor. Like my dear Lucy. There is nothing sweeter. And yet..."

His grip slid down my arm, to my hand—squeezing, forcing me to release my grip on the bottle. It fell, scattering pills across the hardwood.

"Tainted. Like you have done to so many others."

"I-I treat very sick patients, Vlad. Medication is an invaluable—"

"Yes, but many are not *very sick*, only weary. Or overwhelmed. Or lonely. And those... *ahh, those* are the ones *I* can treat. But not after they've met with you." His breath chilled my neck. "No, after one session, you've poisoned them. Made them useless. Both to me and to themselves."

His lifeless lips brushed against my jaw, and death scraped down my spine.

I sat paralyzed but managed to choke out a plea. "Don't. I don't want your help. I'll find another way. I'll stop the pills, for myself and for any patients that don't absolutely need them."

A grim, mirthless chuckle. "Oh, don't worry, Doctor. You are in no danger."

Those words brought a flicker of hope, a moment of clarity. "So... So you *have* changed."

"Yes, as blood slowly drains from a wound, I too have changed."

"I-Is there no chance to heal that wound?"

"For me? No."

Suddenly, the light returned, and I sat alone with the storm howling through my open window. I glanced down at my scattered pills and slumped back in my chair, Vlad's final words sighing in the wind.

"But for you..."

HEART OF MADNESS

Erin Artfitch

"Your six o'clock is here, Dr. Sutton."

Winnefred Sutton's aging receptionist stood halfway through the office threshold. Despite the woman's repeated and increasingly irate protests, Win was fairly certain Gladys knew how to use the intercom system. She just didn't.

Win eyed the new deck of cards on her desk wistfully. She ached to escape to her cozy loft on the east side of London. To spend the remainder of the evening playing solitaire with her cat happily purring upon her lap. But, alas, one last patient required her services.

Past the old woman, Win's client sat in a wingback leather chair, twisting the arm with a knuckle-white grip. A tangled mass of blonde locks hid the teenager's face, and a baby-blue sweater swallowed her fragile frame.

Odd...

Like the outdated, stuffy furniture and even Gladys, Win had "inherited" this client three years ago when she'd taken over her late father's psychiatric practice. Typically, they met every Tuesday.

This visit was... unexpected. Clearly, something had rattled her.

A sinking suspicion tightened Win's chest, and she fished a

file from her desk drawer. "Tell her I'll be with her momentarily."

Gladys didn't bother to close the door, instead shuffling away at a snail's pace.

Win scanned her client's file, skimming the information she already knew.

Diagnosis: Post-Traumatic Stress Disorder.

Patient suffers from frequent, recurring night terrors...

Paranoid delusions...

Win inhaled sharply when she found it. The date of the accident. November 1st, 2014. Nine years ago, to the day.

No wonder the girl looked devastated.

Win took a steadying breath. "Come in."

Her client walked as if the floors were made of glass. She nudged the office door shut with the heel of her sneaker and sat in the chair across from Win.

"I noticed the date," Win said gently. "Is that why you've come?"

Startlingly blue eyes met hers. Eyes filled with fear. "It's happening again, Dr. Sutton."

"What, darling?"

"The visions. I... I'm seeing them again."

It was normal for patients to regress around the anniversary of their traumatic event, but Win didn't voice that. "The night terrors?"

"No—I mean, yes. Always. But... I'm hearing voices during the day now." She looked around, as if her invisible tormentors were in the room at the very moment. "And I'm... seeing things."

Win stiffened. During the girl's childhood, she had breaks with reality, triggered by certain sounds, smells, or places. This was a deep regression.

"What are you seeing?" Win asked, careful to keep her voice conversational.

The girl's hands clenched. She shook her head. "Crazy things.

I saw a caterpillar at the park. He spoke to me. He told me I was in danger. That *she* is looking for me again."

Heavens, this was more than a simple regression. Her client had slipped into full hallucinations.

"She's sending her scouts for me. I can hear her beast's call. It's screaming—"

"Alice!" Win's voice was sharper than she'd intended it to be, but the girl stopped. Looked at her with wide eyes.

"It's not real, darling. You must believe that." Win leaned forward and gave what she hoped was a reassuring smile. "Focus on what is. Nine years ago today, you chased a rabbit and fell into a well. You were trapped for days. The hole flooded. You survived on mushrooms, which, frankly, probably made your experience that much more confusing. You coped with this very real trauma by creating a safer fantasy world. Wonderland."

Win hoped she was getting through, but oddly enough though, Alice looked pensive instead of stark raving mad.

"Dr. Sutton, this feels different," she insisted. "When I followed the white rabbit, I traveled from this world to Wonderland. Now most of the voices are coming from..." Alice's gaze lifted to the gilded mirror hanging above Win's desk. "The mirrors. I can hear them inside the mirrors. Sometimes, if I look long enough, I think I can *see* them. The rabbit with his watch. The hatter. The Cheshire cat and his funny smile."

Alice's cheeks reddened, as if ashamed by her own words. Yet she almost sounded wistful.

Her eyes narrowed on the deck of cards on Win's desk. She paled. "Did you—did you see that?"

Win straightened. "See what?"

"That Queen of Hearts just winked at me. She just moved!" Alice scrambled from her chair, nearly knocking it over.

Cold spiders crept along Win's spine. She rose as well. "Alice,

I think we might try some medication. Just to get you through these next few days, hmm?"

The girl stared at the cards. "What if I'm not mad? What if it's all real?"

Win walked briskly to her filing cabinet and pulled it open. She'd just ordered a new prescription pad. Where was it?

Behind her, Alice shuffled. Most likely moving to the mirror, the poor girl. Win prayed this episode was merely severe anxiety. If her mental health kept deteriorating, they would need to discuss alternative, long-term treatments. Finally, Win clasped her new script pad. She turned back to an empty room. Win took a cautious step forward. "Alice?"

Odd. She hadn't heard the door open.

Win peeked into the reception area. "Gladys, did my client leave?"

The crone looked up from her ancient desktop, eyebrows shooting to her permed gray curls. "No."

Win closed the door again. She checked under her desk before crossing the room to the window—just for good measure. Locked.

Then she saw them. The deck of cards Alice had been staring at. The Queen of Hearts was missing, leaving behind only a blank card. She thumbed through the deck and found all the heart cards missing.

Win raised her gaze to the mirror and thought she saw the shadow of a girl inside.

Impossible.

She lunged for Alice's file, desperate to call her guardians, when another name caught her attention. Wendy. A girl who claimed she'd been whisked away to an island in the sky. Pure madness. And yet...

Alice's words echoed. *What if it's all real?*

THE BLACK BLIZZARD

Andrea Renae

"I've got a good feeling about you, Planet 77."

My heart thundered with the anticipation of facing the water-hungry nightmare that had buried our planet. Our ship slowed as we breached the skies of Earth.

"Don't forget the cloaking device." Jones reached over my shoulder and flipped a toggle. "I'd rather not be deified this time."

I kept my eyes forward, trying to act as calm as he was. My partner swung a leg over his chair and sat. A data panel glowed between his hands.

"Hm. Your figure *was* extremely striking cast in Antaxxin gold." I glanced at him, craving his comedic response like a drug, but his brow pinched.

"Abbi, this is it." His gray-blue eyes found mine. "This is where it's been hiding."

I squinted at the wisps of cloud, as tame as Maulturian meringues. Discouragement flared in my chest. "Not a chance." Our planet's ravaged skies, which we had left behind three years ago, looked nothing like Earth's.

The copilot's chair squeaked as Jones rested the data panel in my palms, then tapped the screen. "*Look at it,* would you?"

A sharp inhale parted my lips. The pictures of black clouds

blotting out the sun dredged up the memories that had driven us across five galaxies. They were irrefutable evidence of the planet-burying alien parasite. But I'd never seen such archaic black-and-white photos of the terrestrial Tempestia's billows before. "*How...*"

"I tweaked the search parameters to include all weather phenomena in Earth's history." When I raised an eyebrow, he shrugged. "I also had a sense about this place. They called it 'the Dust Bowl.' In the 1930s all the area's farmlands were reduced to... well, dust."

"Impossible." We'd chased every rumored Tempestic event across seventy-six planets, but there was never any indication that they were capable of time travel. Until now.

Jones squeezed my shoulder. "Abbi, please trust me. I've got a gut feeling."

"That's indigestion."

He huffed and tightened his grip until I looked at him. "This thing... it's been plaguing Earth for years."

Years? I closed my eyes, picturing the soft, turquoise plains I'd roamed as a child. The image shifted into seas of grit under a red sky. My mouth went dry—I could still feel the impossible thirst. Would that be Earth's fate too?

I flicked my hand across the data panel, sending both the physical and temporal coordinates to the ship. It plunged us beneath the cloud layer with breathtaking speed.

"Could you not have waited until we were buckled in?" Jones yelped, and I allowed myself a small laugh.

Miles and centuries disappeared in a blur. The approaching cities seemed to fold in on themselves as we threw their timelines into reverse. When we reached the programmed decade, a familiar filthy blizzard swallowed our ship.

Jones let out a low whistle. "Welcome to Black Sunday."

Our cloaking tech was unnecessary since the massive dust storm reduced our vision to a handful of feet in all directions. The ship landed in an empty field, and Jones and I went to the loading bay. My hands shook as he strapped the neutralizer to his back.

"All we gotta do is get close enough to activate this thing, then get out of the way." He grabbed two full-face respirator masks, which would filter out the suffocating dust. I snapped mine on and set the thermal imagers to visualize the alien Tempestia. Steeling myself, I turned to Jones.

"Whatever happens, I want you to know that I lo—"

He grabbed my hand and lowered the hatch before I could finish.

I had forgotten just how wicked the Tempestia was. It towered a hundred feet, whipping dozens of limbs out from its twisted body. Sensitive probes designed to siphon moisture from the atmosphere covered every inch of its flesh. And that's just what the Tempestia would do—suck the entire planet dry.

We only made it twenty yards before it spotted us. The alien pointed its hideous arms, and the storm became a solid mass directed solely at us.

The wind nearly ripped my mask off, and as I struggled to hold it there was a cry. I turned. An airborne piece of debris hit Jones with a sickening *crunch*, ripping him from my grip and launching him into the churning filth.

I ran to him and crumpled at his side. He had lost his mask, and though I shook him, he would not wake.

"Don't you dare leave me," I sobbed, tears splattering my mask.

The beast roared, and memories of my city entombed under mountains of silt pressed clarity into my mind. There was no way I could drag Jones back to the ship. I rolled him over and fumbled to unbuckle the neutralizer, then slipped my arms into its straps.

I faced the Tempestia.

And charged.

Pebbles lacerated my exposed skin, and my feet barely stayed on the ground. The monster screamed, and I screamed back.

"Not today, you devil!"

Throwing the pack off my back, I punched the switch and spun, letting the Tempestia's winds push me out of the neutralizer's radius.

The device's deafening pulse ripped through the air, throwing me aside. A dome of energy spread through the sky. I gasped in relief—I was on the outside. The gale within became perfectly still under the immobilizing effect of the neutralizer. The trapped Tempestia writhed as it consumed every molecule of moisture, suffocating itself. Crumbling to dust.

I collapsed on the dirt drifts and ripped off my respirator. The sky grew bluer and bluer by the second, and I couldn't contain my tears. Earth was safe, and my planet was avenged.

"See? Definitely not indigestion."

My heart leapt. Jones was battered, but he managed to crawl over and rest his head in my lap. A smile tugged at my lips as I brushed dirt off his brow.

"I told you I had a good feeling about Planet 77."

GALES OF SONG

Rose Q. Addams

A stroke here, a line there... Painful memories wash away beneath the ethereal beauty my brush brings to pass. I lean back to observe my work—the feathery swirls across the glass—and touch up one corner. I love creating this, even if it melts away within minutes of sunrise.

Sometimes, I'd swear my brush was guided by something other than my own hand, but I know for a fact it isn't ensorcelled. I'll never again touch an enchanted object, if I have a choice in the matter. Nor could the mysterious guiding be the influence of another, for the impassive moon, the wind, and I are the only ones who would brave a night this cold.

The wind tugs at my sleeve, and I sweep it away. "Not now."

It tugs again, and I frown. "I'm not done."

It whistles around my head, irritable and insistent, and I sigh, rising from my midair crouch. "All right, all right. What is it?"

Cheery swirling, tittering. Blasted breeze knows when it's won.

"If you don't show me, I'll just finish my painting."

It grows remarkably still, and as I open my mouth to ask why, a little gust appears from the distance, bringing with it a faint echo of a single note.

Most peculiar, indeed. The wind is rarely enamored of any music but its own… and who'd be awake on a night like this? Most Men are eager to sleep through winter nights this cold and crisp, and few Fey know, or can unlock, the Ways into the mortal realm.

Of course, "few" doesn't mean *none*. So I tuck my brush back into my waistcoat pocket and follow the wind as it rushes toward that distant note. The smaller breezes dart back and forth, ruffling my hair and tugging me onward as I stride over the gales. The note is joined by another as they dart off and return, and soon the song grows into a complex melody without words.

The vocalizations come from still farther, and the wind soon begins to sing along, accenting and complementing the voice as it rises full and free.

Something in the song draws me onward, even when the wind flies ahead, and I should by all rights lose interest. It just seems… right, like one of my completed pictures on a stranger's window. I run faster to catch up with the wind, leaving the habitations of Men far behind.

We cross the borders of the No-Man's Land that skirts the Northern Wastes—my old home.

A shiver runs down my spine. I would turn back, if it weren't for the siren call of that song. I must find its source, whatever the cost. Mercifully, we turn east, flying through No-Man's Land until I spot a tower tucked amongst the ancient trees that fill a sheltered valley, almost as if the builder wanted to keep it from the world. The voice is stronger here, notes undulating smoothly as the winds fall still in hushed awe.

To keep from disturbing the singer, I alight on the roof as lightly as possible, and I creep down to the edge.

The voice below rings on, each note pure as silver.

I grasp the edge of the roof and look downward, willing myself hidden from sight... for now.

The song continues uninterrupted, and I lean farther, pulse quickening. I haven't had my curiosity piqued this much in centuries. The magnetic pull of the voice is irresistible.

The singer seems barely more than a girl. But as she turns her head upward, looking through me to the stars, I catch my breath. She's a beautiful woman, though young. Her eyes catch the starlight and throw it back as her song bubbles outward. Her skin is alabaster, her lips as pink as a rose, and her hair...

Her hair is impossibly long. Coiled about her head, draped down around her on the window-seat, it falls like a golden river. Some trails into the darkness behind her, and some falls out of the window for the littlest breezes to play with.

I cannot help but stare as her song seems to draw to a close. Then, to my surprise, she renews the tune and slowly forms words, as though pulling them from the depths of the song itself.

Let us sing back, let us sing,
For the song is eternal.
We are not its Maker—
He rejoices o'er us in singing.

Finally, she goes still, and she reaches out as though to touch the sky. "I suppose it was silly. But..." She closes her eyes and lets out a sigh. "Goodnight, anyway."

She looks up again, a sad smile on her lips. Who *is* this, and why should she set my heart pounding?

The breezes, surprisingly, gently reach out and brush her face, and she closes her eyes with another gentle smile. "And goodnight to you, too," she says to the gust, which, elated that she's noticed it, rushes about, then up to me, buzzing with joy. I hold a finger to my lips, and it settles. An idea sparks, and I wait until she's closed the window before I dare to shift.

She draws the curtains, and all goes still. I leap down, landing lightly on the air itself, and draw my brush from its place. I relax, color seeping back into me as I release my hiding spell to focus. Somehow, I know she'll rise early, so I work quickly.

As I press brush to glass, the frost grows across the surface in swirls and curlicues that grow more ornate as I focus on the notes her voice carried.

I don't paint to forget, this time. Perhaps she'll see it and be made happy. Perhaps she'll never notice it, as most Men don't. But I'll leave it here, a gift to her, as her song was to me.

I sign my work, as I always do, with a faint flourish.

Jack Frost.

THE SANTA DILEMMA

Nate Swanson

Santa knew this house. As his sleigh bumped lightly on the slate roof, he noticed a Frisbee nestled in a gutter. *I gave that to Suzy last year.* Santa bent down, his ample belly bending easily, and tossed the toy into the yard. He liked the girl here, but her brother Bobby was next level.

Frowning in thought, Santa put a hand on the chimney. Bobby was a technical whiz kid, and his Santa detection schemes were some of the best. *This year won't be any easier.* Maybe after turning fourteen he'd lost faith in "The Jolly Fat Man," but Santa hoped not. This kid *believed*, and that was both a blessing and a danger.

Sighing, Santa grabbed his utility belt and swung it around his ample waist—it held everything the smart anti-burglar would need for an incursion. Saying a quick prayer, he jumped down the chimney.

As he neared the bottom, he used his extra-stick boots to brake himself. Just as he'd expected, Bobby had a GoPro pointed up the chimney right at him. The boy had even painted the camera white to match the nearby birch logs. Santa hung in deep shadow, but that would mask his approach only so far. Santa pulled a small chunk of freeze-dried soot from a pouch and expertly dropped it on the lens.

LEGENDARY

He unclipped his Flexible Energy Detection Utility Project—FED-UP—and slid the antenna around the bottom of the opening. His best tech elves had given him the tool four years ago; it could spot listening devices, spy cameras, and Wi-Fi signals. It picked up six gadgets and some solid Wi-Fi. Santa grabbed his Disposable Internet Serial Signal Energy Disruptor, set the channel, and stuck it inside the chimney with a four-minute self-destruct timer. He hoped Dad and Mom were asleep for the evening. While this disabled the offending cameras and mics, their internet would also be offline.

"Okay, Bobby," Santa whispered. He slid down the rest of the way, boots thumping quietly on the ground. "It's *mano a mano* now."

Scanning the living room, he detected some old-school traps, probably set by the younger sister, Suzy—yarn pulled between chairs and tied up with bells, scattered Legos, and cookies that, if taken, would drop a cardboard box on the snacker. Santa deftly stepped through the room, avoiding each snare. After hundreds of years on the job, the motions were child's play.

Cookies, then the tree, or the other way around? Santa always tried to keep it fresh. *Cookies first.* He approached the counter, stepping over Lego pieces and more twine. He scrutinized the cookies. A tiny bit of plastic peeked out from under one sugary morsel. *Tricky.* Taking one of the others, he sighed and popped it into his mouth.

Now for the tree. Santa reversed course and silently stepped over to the white spruce, nicely decorated in midcentury modern style. As he did, he glanced at his escape route.

And froze.

Red laser lines crisscrossed the fireplace opening. How had that happened? Had he missed something, or was it on a timer? He unclipped his tablet and pulled up the house blueprints. The breaker box was in the parents' closet upstairs.

Santa put the tree between him and the rest of the room, quickly placing the presents. He slid over to the fireplace and filled the stockings, taking extra pleasure in dropping a hunk of coal into Bobby's sock. Santa was going to step away when he remembered the whole self-esteem thing. So, he returned and put the other items in Bobby's stocking, leaving the coal in place. Santa heard feet shuffle in the upstairs hallway. Turning, he ducked back behind the tree.

Santa peeked through the spruce branches. A sleepy fourteen-year-old face appeared in the doorway. Bobby's eyes lit up, and he pumped his fist up and down. Wincing, he looked backward, clearly afraid to wake his parents. As Bobby turned his head, Santa considered his choices: should he stay hidden or move? He sprinted through the den door and pressed his ample body against the wall.

Bobby wandered right past Santa's hiding place, bent down to examine the presents under the tree, then walked over to the fireplace. The young menace to Santa's mystique looked at the stockings, then checked the laser grid. As he was occupied, Santa slid around the wall and tiptoed to the top of the stairs.

The best way to get out is always the simplest. It was so tempting to go for the breaker box and take down a large portion of Bobby's arsenal. However... Palming one more item from his belt, Santa chose the path of humility. Tiptoeing to Bobby's bedroom door, he opened it, revealing a clean room. *Good boy, Bobby. Maybe you'll keep your position on the Nice List next year.*

Santa silently pulled the window open, slapped the gadget in his palm onto the sash bead, and slid the window shut behind him. Then, pulling himself up on the rooftop, he winked at his reindeer and hopped into his sleigh, yelling, "Merry Christmas to all, and to all a good night!"

Santa's Child Activity Detection System lit up like a Christmas tree as Bobby sprinted up the stairs. He tugged on the window, but the Six-Minute Automatic Release Tape Santa had placed there held firm.

Santa flew out of sight, laughing. "Well played, Bobby. Well played."

WANT MORE?

Visit gohavok.com for a free story every weekday. Or better yet, join the *Havok Horde* for chances to win reader prizes and the opportunity to vote on the Readers' Choice story for each anthology. Membership is only $4.99 per year and includes access to the ever-growing archive of stories (over 1,500 at last count!).

See the **Havok Flash Fiction** series on Amazon.com to purchase.

DID YOU ENJOY THIS BOOK?

Please consider leaving a review on Amazon and Goodreads (and your blog, social media, and anywhere else you'd like... maybe a tattoo?) and show our authors some love. Let them know which stories you enjoyed most!

ABOUT OUR AUTHORS

Author names are listed alphabetically by last name.

Rose Q. Addams loves cheesecake, hats, and her family, whom she blames for her love of reading. Some of her best memories are hearing tales of Heidi, Winnie the Pooh, Beauty and The Beast, and the prophet Ehud—which explains how her taste runs wildly throughout genres. She can be found scribbling madly on any paper she gets and praising her Savior for the weird and wonderful things in her life. // rewriteswithafaeriepen.wordpress.com

Elizabeth Arceo's love for storytelling began with reading Narnia as a child. Ever since, she's told stories through any medium, whether words, music, or paint. Elizabeth has written articles for Myra Leana and edited stories for Pensacola Christian College. Besides writing, Elizabeth can be found knee-deep in acrylics, violin, illustration, heavy novels, martial arts, and ASL practice. She lives in "Sin City" Las Vegas—a half-hour away from the chaos.

Erin Artfitch had three goals as a teenager: become a writer, get married and raise some lil' bookworms, and acquire superpowers. She's still working on the superpowers part (though she's pretty sure keeping up with laundry for four humans qualifies). Erin reads and writes speculative books with unique worlds and surprise endings. // erinartfitch.com

Deborah Bainbridge is a Christian, wife, and mother who enjoys running, traveling the world, writing short stories, and cookies. She is always ready for an adventure! She dedicates this lighthearted story to her brilliant, spectacular son, Skylar, who sported a red chinstrap beard in high school and is filled with good-hearted leprechaun shenanigans. She is thankful to her family and friends for their encouragement, feedback, and inspiration.

Emily Barnett lives in the mountains with her husband and hobbit sons. Her whimsical and poignant stories have been published in several anthologies and online magazines. Emily's flash fiction piece, "Sky Rays," was a Realm Maker's finalist in 2023, and her YA fantasy debut, *Thread of Dreams*, was published March 2024. // emilybarnettauthor.com

P. J. Benjamin writes a blog called *The Firmament* which explores the intersection between good fiction and better theology. While his creative passion is for weaving sound biblical doctrine into his work, his greatest joy is in helping other speculative fiction writers do the same. He lives with his wife in the scenic Pacific Northwest, spending his free time cooking, bladesmithing, and accumulating more board games than he has time to play. // pjbenjamin.net

Hannah Carter is just a girl who wakes up every day hoping it will be the day she discovers she's secretly a mermaid. Her debut novel, *Depths of Atlantis*, is out through SnowRidge Press now. Her stories have been included in several anthologies: *Whispers From Before*, *The Never Tales*, and Havok's *Casting Call* and *Prismatic*. Her flash fiction piece, "A Home for Nova," won the 2022 Flash Fiction Realm Award. // introvertedmermaid3.mailerpage.com

Teddi Deppner is an indie author, enthusiastic encourager of other creatives, and 20+ year veteran of the tech and marketing world. She enjoys science fiction and urban fantasy the most but never lets genre stop her from diving into a good story. // teddideppner.com

Jim Doran is a genre writer who enjoys transporting his readers to unique destinations filled with wonder… or danger. Whether it's the fairytale hijinks in his Kingdom Fantasy series or his multi-genre short stories, Jim aims to entertain his audience with every word. When he's not writing, he's usually enjoying the seasons in Michigan. His website contains illustrations from his Havok stories. // jimdorantales.com

J. L. Ender is the author of the superhero series Steel Fox Investigations, as well as a number of other novels and short stories. Ender has worked as a dishwasher, a beef jerky labeler, a warehouse worker, a shelf stocker, a greeter, a traveling technician, a laser engraver, a package handler, a copywriter, a graphic designer, a librarian, an editor, a dispatcher, a phone operator, a hotel clerk, and hopefully someday soon as a novelist… He lives in Ohio with his wife and fellow writer SCE Ender. // enderauthor.wixsite.com/mysite

Gretchen E. K. Engel writes steampunk and urban fantasy she describes as "real world setting with a supernatural twist." When she's not writing, she researches STEM characters in a professional setting and gets paid to do it. She has published short stories in anthologies and magazines. Gretchen lives in Tucson with her husband, daughter, and cat, plus her college student son across town. She enjoys tennis, running, biking, hiking, traveling, or lying on a pool float doing nothing. // gretchenekengel.com

Abigail Falanga may be found in New Mexico creating magic in many ways—with fabric, food, paper, music, and especially with words! She's loved fantasy ever since playing out epic adventures of swords, fairies, and monsters with her siblings, and loved sci-fi since her dad's stories around the dinner table. Besides sharing mad little stories on Havok, she is busily trying to launch approximately five hundred novels into the world. Some of them are even finished! // abigailfalangaauthor.wordpress.com

Winnifred Fritz is a homeschool mom with a passion for reading, writing, and playing video games with her husband and kids. Winnifred, Fred to her friends, was often scolded as a child for daydreaming and now puts her imagination to good use, crafting speculative stories with unusual characters and compelling themes of finding family, redemption, and overcoming fears.

Jeff Gard is an assistant professor of English at Briar Cliff University in Sioux City, Iowa. When he isn't writing or teaching, he enjoys board games, disc golf, binge-worthy television shows, music, and procrastination (see above). Many of his fiction ideas arise from random thoughts that strike in the middle of the night when he should be asleep. His stories have appeared in *Every Day Fiction, The Arcanist, Daily Science Fiction,* and *Flash Fiction Magazine.* // jeffgardfiction.wordpress.com

Ronnell Kay Gibson specializes in contemporary fiction with a sprinkling of the fantastical. She also writes youth and adult devotions and is one of the editors for Havok Publishing. Self-proclaimed coffee snob and Marvel movie addict, Ronnell has also titled herself a macaron padawan and a cupcake Jedi. High on her bucket list is to attend San Diego Comic Con. Ronnell lives in central Wisconsin with her husband and two Pomeranian puppies. // ronnellkaygibson.com

Sophia L. Hansen writes organically, using no hormones, antibiotics, or pesticides on her words unless it's absolutely convenient. She's lived on a tiny island in Alaska, the bustling cities of New York and Boston, and has settled in the Southeast where she writes and edits *In Other Worlds*. She is an editor with Havok Publishing and her debut novel, *Water's Break*, was released early in January 2024. Sophia loves plenty of coffee, crispy bacon, and that—after 30+ years of marriage, seven children, and numerous pets—she can still fit into her high school earrings. // sophialhansen.com

Rachel Ann Michael Harris is a writer of middle grade fantasy stories (most of the time). She has an eclectic taste in stories which transfers to her writing, working in various genres. She has been published in several anthologies, with Havok, and is the author of *The Beauty of Magic*. // rachelannmichaelharris.com

Andrew Hayes & Daniel Gomez are both freshmen students at St. Stephen's Academy. Andrew enjoys riding horses, leading his scout troop, and playing *The Legend of Zelda* video game series. Daniel likes reading, drinking coffee, and also enjoys video games. Both Andrew and Daniel took a creative writing class and have both enjoyed their growth in poem and story writing.

Kat Heckenbach graduated from the University of Tampa with a bachelor's degree in biology, went on to teach math, and then homeschooled her son and daughter while writing and making sci-fi/fantasy art. She is the author of the YA fantasy series Toch Island Chronicles and urban fantasy *Relent*, as well as dozens of fantasy, science fiction, and horror short stories in magazines and anthologies. Enter her world at her website. // katheckenbach.com

Laurie Herlich loves living in rural northeast Tennessee, where Story is everything. She writes flash fiction and cozy mysteries in a converted garden hut situated in her backyard. Laurie is a regular contributor to ChristianDevotions.us and won a 2023 Selah Award in the online devotion category, as well as a first place 2023 Foundation Award for her unpublished novella. She is also a contributor/performer for Jonesborough, Tennessee's *StoryTown* NPR Radio Show/Podcast, and is a StoryTeller with the Jonesborough Storytelling Guild.

A people-loving introvert, **Lauren Hildebrand** can never talk enough about old books or Jesus Christ. She lives in always-windy Kansas, considers Asian cuisine a primary food group, and can usually be found devouring classics or planning her next cosplay. As a writer, Lauren loves to tell stories that mingle humor, hardship, and hope. As a fiction editor, her passion is encouraging and teaching young writers. She works as an editor with Havok Publishing and is an instructor at the Author Conservatory.

Hailey Huntington is a speculative fiction author, penning tales of wonder, hope, and heroes, with a dash of wit. Her stories can be found online and in various print anthologies. When not writing or reading, Hailey can be found listening to her favorite film scores, making homemade ice cream, or spending time with her family. // haileyhuntington.com

S. M. Jake is an author of fantasy stories for those who love adventure, family, dad-jokes, wonder, and weird stuff. She draws inspiration from fairy tales and tall tales, and will take every opportunity to add a touch of the Midwest to her writing. Her other loves include her husband and two boys, their MCM house, singing at church, spotty gardening, and chaos sewing clothing on ridiculous deadlines. // smjake.com

Kevin King enjoys Renaissance Fairs, bookstores, fencing, and daydreaming. He has been reading fantasy from age six, and writing from age twenty-two. He loves exploring fantasy worlds, especially exploring human nature through fiction. Fantasy is his first love, but he also dabbles in sci-fi, creepy horror, and devastatingly sad dramas. // kevinkingauthor.com

Rachel Lawrence writes stories and poetry about the everyday joys and challenges of life, love, and choosing the perfect snack food for every occasion. She draws inspiration from her experience growing up in a huge family in the Carolinas and having her views expanded by new friends and family she's met along the way, both at home and across the ocean. She's a wife, mom, and lover of inside jokes. She plays Christmas music year-round.

Jenneth Leed spent her childhood hunting ghosts and searching for secret passages (both inside and outside of a good book). As an adult, she found an actual secret door in an actually haunted tavern and now considers her life complete. In addition to writing, Jenneth loves designing book covers for independent authors and watching heist shows. She currently resides near Washington D.C. and holds an MA in graphic design. // jennethdyck.wordpress.com

Pamela Love was born in New Jersey and worked as a teacher and in marketing before becoming a writer. Her work has appeared in Havok, *Page & Spine*, and *Luna Station Quarterly*. She is the 2020 winner of the Magazine Merit Fiction Award for her story "The Fog Test," which appeared in *Cricket*. She and her family live in Maryland.

Morgan J. Manns is a speculative fiction writer who firmly believes that the world needs more stories filled with magic and wonder. Captivated by the realm of intricate world-building since composing her first fantasy tale at the age of ten, she now ventures beneath the endless Canadian prairie sky with her supportive husband and two hobbit children, all while eagerly contemplating her next literary creation. While her current occupation is that of an elementary school teacher, her dream job will always be dragon rider, soaring through the skies of her imaginings.

Rebecca Morgan began her writing journey by scribbling on a page—and being incredibly proud of her "stories." Years later, she has had several works of short fiction published with Havok. Rebecca aims to write stories that show healing through the power of story and help the brokenhearted. Besides writing, Rebecca loves the works of J.R.R. Tolkien, cooking, blue oceans, salsa, and all things apothecary. // authorrebeccamorgan.com

Elizabeth Anne Myrick lives in Kansas City with a golden retriever named Edith, a suitcase named Posey, and several houseplants with unfortunately forgotten names (but she swears there's a Kenneth in there somewhere). Always hungry for adventure, she's visited sixteen real-world countries and countless fictional ones. Her stories glimmer with hope and a sprinkle of magic. You can find Elizabeth on the back deck with her iced coffee or on Instagram as @eamyrick. // elizabethannemyrick.com

R. L. Nguyen is a child of immigrant parents who found her place to belong in fictional worlds. Her classical education and studies at the Author Conservatory feed her quest after truth and beauty. When she's not writing magical characters finding victory in darkness, she can be found reading Shakespeare, singing opera, and training her dogs in rural South Carolina.

Karyne Norton hasn't found the key to time travel, immortality, or infinite lives, so she's taking a break from nursing and photography to focus on raising four human beings while writing epic fantasy. Her debut novel, *Blood of the Stars*, released in March 2024. When she's not writing, she's reading, which is why she's also the host of the *Finding Fantasy Reads* podcast, where she reads a new short story every week from a variety of fantasy authors. // karynenorton.com

Maia Rebekah is an SNHU graduate, an aspiring copy editor/proofreader, and a staff member at Havok Publishing. She's a roller-coaster junkie who loves reading and writing Christian sci-fi/fantasy, hiking, playing board games, and listening to outdated Christian rock.

Lincoln Reed is a writer, filmmaker, and professor. He holds an MFA in creative writing from Miami University (OH). More than sixty of his short stories are featured in online publications and print anthologies. The short film adaptations of his Havok stories "Tritanopia" and "Dark Side of the Moon" have screened at film festivals across the United States, Australia, Spain, Mexico, and Iceland. // lincolnreedonline.com

Andrea Renae grew up wandering the Canadian prairies with a cat in tow. An only child, she thrilled in stories of all kinds. Writing became a way to process life's countless beauties, hardships, and oddities. She can often be found playing piano, experimenting with watercolors, knitting sweaters, or practicing for her inevitable fame on the GBBO. Her heart will always be with her family, her friends, and her goofy goldendoodle. // authorarenae.com

Victoria Roberts has been making up stories in her head for as long as she can remember. She writes uplifting Sonflower Stories that radiate light. When she's not penning or devouring a new tale, she spends her time adventuring with her husband, spoiling their poodle Beast, or creating book-themed cross-stitch patterns. // victoriaroberts-author.com

Mia Rumi is a lover of stories and their power to comfort and inspire. She enjoys writing fiction, particularly fantasy. One of her first memories as a writer involves sitting on the floor and writing a story about two pandas with her older sister. She loves tea, Irish moss, and the smell of old books.

Kez Sharrow is an emergent unicorn living in Wuhan. By day she dabbles in the alchemy of human transformation as a leadership coach. Early mornings and weekends, she creates worlds out of smoke and dragon's breath. Kez belongs to the tribe of the uprooted and transplanted, those who live between cultures, and she writes stories of travelers in fantasy worlds. // kezsharrow.com

Nate Swanson is a software engineer by trade but an author in his bones. Living in the rural Central Valley of California keeps him grounded while living near Silicon Valley keeps him dreaming. Nate finds that he loves noble, beautiful, and honorable things that start ugly and small. It is in the metamorphosis from one to the other that he finds his favorite subject matter. Nate loves writing in the LitRPG genre and is publishing his first novel as a weekly serial on Royal Road while working on his second. // sanctifyingescape.com

Michael Teasdale is an English author whose stories have appeared for a variety of publications including *Shoreline of Infinity* and *Wyldblood*. As well as appearing in a number of Havok anthologies, his work can also be found in books by World Weaver Press, Tyche Books, and Air and Nothingness Press. He lives in Transylvania, Romania, with three beloved cats and is an associate member of the SFWA.

Rachael Watson has spent her whole life hopelessly lost in the world of stories. From a sobbing sixteen-year-old finishing *The Return of the King* by J. R. R. Tolkien, to dancing on stage professionally, to creating bespoke adventures for her children, she enjoys pulling on the imaginative strings of "what-ifs" to see where the unraveling takes her. Rachael drinks her coffee black but loves a milky cuppa Yorkshire tea.

When **Andrew Winch**, PT, isn't mending bones as a physical therapist, he's breaking them as an author. From flash fiction to novels, Andrew writes action-packed science fiction that keeps you guessing. He's also the editor-in-chief for Havok Publishing, a father, and a bunch of other things, which you can read all about on his website. // raisingsupergirl.com

Havok will return in Season 11...
"Remember When"

Made in United States
North Haven, CT
29 March 2025